# The
# Tidal Space
# Between

**Also by Cassandra Stirling**

Space Between Urban Fantasy Series
*The Deep Space Between*
*The Dark Space Between*

Merryton Mews Cozy Mystery Series
*Poisons and Pens*
*Holly and Havoc*

# THE TIDAL

# SPACE

# BETWEEN

CASSANDRA STIRLING

For more information and to sign up for my newsletter, visit
https://cassandracstirling.com/spacebetween-book0.

Cover art by Getcovers.com.

THE TIDAL SPACE BETWEEN

ISBN 979-8-9867520-0-6 *Paperback*
ISBN 979-8-9867520-1-3 *Ebook*

*To Millie and Maddie, two of the most amazing young people I know.
I can't wait to see where the world takes you.*

# Contents

*"Close friends are truly life's treasures. Sometimes they know us better than we know ourselves. With gentle honesty, they are there to guide and support us, to share our laughter and our tears. Their presence reminds us that we are never really alone."*
— Vincent van Gogh

# 1

## THE ARRIVAL

### (It Was Not All Fun and Games)

Seraphina Lastra Covington twirled her hair around her fingers as the smell of the ocean overtook the SUV. The closer they got to her best friend's house in the Hamptons, the stronger it became. She bet it was Ro letting her Selkie side out, rather than the glimpses of the Atlantic peeking between the trees.

Ro burst out laughing, and Seraphina smiled, asking, "What's so funny?"

"It's this thing. Lance said what now and Daisy replied, and then Lance…" Ro's voice trailed off. "There's too much." Ro's grin brightened as she tapped out a response on her phone.

The smile slid from Seraphina's face as she tugged harder on her hair. "Oh. Okay."

That'd been happening a lot this year. Inside jokes she wasn't a part of. Parties she wasn't invited to. New friends, like Lance and Daisy, who Ro had mocked before.

"Wow," Ro said.

"What?"

"Daisy's decided on Stanford. She's spending the summer working on her mom, so there's no roadblocks."

Seraphina hoped Daisy got her wish and got as far away from them as possible. Daisy was one of her main tormentors at school, but only when Ro wasn't around. Which was most of the time lately.

Seraphina tugged on her hair too hard, banging her head on the window. "Ouch," she said as she rubbed the sore spot. "Why would her mom stop her?"

"Everyone in their family went to Brown or Yale. Daisy's breaking tradition. And tradition can be powerful."

Surprised by how bitter Ro sounded, Seraphina asked, "Are traditions binding you, Ro?"

Ro glanced at Dannings in the driver's seat and then gazed back out the window. "Something like that."

Seraphina flicked her gaze between them, a frown on her face. After four years of holidays and summers spent with Ro's family, she was no closer to understanding how the Merrowfolk worked than since her first summer with them. "What do you mean?"

"Nothing."

And... that was why. Any time Seraphina asked a question, Ro shut it down. It happened with more and more frequency. Over the past six months, the gap between them had grown in ways Seraphina had and hadn't expected. She knew they'd stop being roommates when they went to college, but she didn't think that distance creep would happen before they were even out of high school.

The pit of sadness that had become her constant companion since Christmas break tightened in her stomach. The clock ticked louder, and not just on their time together. She wished she had Ro's confidence and ability to know exactly what she wanted and to go for it. But she didn't.

The decisions Seraphina hadn't made gathered like a storm cloud above her head, too nebulous and entangled to pluck one out and slap it down as the right choice. Instead, she had dodged the school counselor meetings about college applications and shrugged whenever teachers asked her.

Growing up sucked.

They turned the final corner, and the house came into view. It reminded her of taffy and laughs, and long conversations on the sand. And hope. One last summer of freedom, hanging out with Ro and talking, with no one else around to get in the way. It would be perfect.

They pulled up next to the front steps and the front door opened as if on cue. Dannings got out before the engine stopped ticking, moving to open Ro's door, but she bounced out before he could. He reversed his course to the trunk for their luggage. Seraphina stepped out and stretched, happy to no longer be stuck in the cramped confines of the back seat.

Dorothy stood on the porch, drying her hands on a towel. "Roslynn, Ms. Lastra, glad to see you've safely arrived. Your rooms are all set if you'd like to freshen up."

"I'm good. I'm dying for a swim. Is anyone about?" Ro said, her tone short as usual when she addressed the housekeeper.

"Your mother is at the club and your father is still in the office, but your brother Jack is here."

"Jack's here?" Ro squealed as she dashed into the house.

Seraphina trailed after her. She didn't know Ro's brother all that well, having only met him for a weekend last summer. He lived and worked in New York City in the Griffith family firm, where they did something with other companies. Ro had never explained, and Seraphina hadn't asked.

"Hello, Ms. Lastra. I've set you up in your usual room, the blue one at the top of the stairs. Dannings will see to the bags."

"Thank you, Dorothy." Seraphina squirmed at the last name Dorothy used to address her. But after two summers, nothing she said would get Dorothy to call her by her dad's last name instead of her mom's. Too long an employee of the Griffiths' and a member of their Merrowfolk colony meant she was a stickler for Magic Community propriety, especially when Ro's grandmother was here.

A shiver ran down Seraphina's spine. Ro swore Beatrice wouldn't be here this year, making Seraphina's choice easy between going home to New Hampshire and the ghosts it held or enjoying summer in the Hamptons with Ro, the beach, and the sun.

Her shoulders hunched as she shoved her hands in her pockets. She hadn't been home since her aunt had dropped her at Harborwood Academy four years ago. She'd have to go back there eventually, but one more summer wouldn't hurt. Besides, it wasn't as if her aunt had protested. The last time they spoke about Seraphina spending another summer with Ro's family, the relief had been palpable in her aunt's voice.

Shaking off her gloomy thoughts, Seraphina followed Ro's excited chatter down the hall to the casual living room on the backside of the house. Large glass windows opened onto the green lawn and the water beyond it. She wandered in, not sure if she should intrude. Ro was weird about her brother.

They wrestled on the sofa, Jack pinning her easily while she shot questions at him.

"What are you doing here? Where's Gemma? How long can you stay? Can you teach me how to drive?" She squirmed under him. "Let me up!"

Jack chuckled and sat back, dodging the pillow Ro aimed at his head. "Gemma's with her family at the Cape, so I'm solo for the summer."

"I never expected to see you! Father said you'd be working at the firm. I'd hoped to do a trip into the city instead and yet here you are." Ro's face split into a huge grin, which Jack mirrored.

For a moment, their similarity was so stark and their joy at being with each other so clear it sliced through Seraphina like a claw through tissue paper. She and her sister Nora would never be like this.

But then Nora had threatened to kill her the last time they spoke. Not exactly close sibling material.

Feeling like an intruder, Seraphina turned to go, but stopped when Jack called out. "Seraphina, right? My ugly sister's poor roommate, who suffers through all her shenanigans?"

Seraphina pivoted on her heel and smiled back at him. "Hi, Jack."

Ro sent another pillow his way. "Shenanigans?! And I am not ugly. I'll have you know half the football team is interested in dating me."

"Yeah, the ugly half."

Ro dove to tackle him again, but he stood up so fast she met only the couch cushions. "Oof."

"Dorothy set you up alright?" he asked to Seraphina, sounding every bit the lord of the manor, like Mr. Bingley in *Pride and Prejudice.*

It didn't help that he reminded her of the actor who had played Bingley in the TV adaptation of the novel. Seraphina blushed and used her hair as a curtain to hide behind. She hadn't remembered how attractive he was. Not that it mattered. Merrowfolk and humans did not mix. None of the phyla did, except in her family.

Jack raised his eyebrows as he waited for a response, and she blushed harder. "Yes, thanks."

"Good." He stepped further away from the couch. "Stop, Ro. You'll have plenty of time to beat me up later."

"Are you here for the entire summer?"

"I am... not sure. But at least for the foreseeable future."

"Oh, good. Let's go for a swim." Ro bounced off the couch, her eyes bluer than the ocean outside the house.

"Alright."

Ro's movement stilled. "Really?"

"Yes, but only for today."

Ro stuck her lower lip out. "Why?"

"Yeah, but only to work with dad on a big deal. And because of the summons."

Ro frowned. "What are you talking about?"

"You didn't hear?"

A warning rippled through Seraphina as his tone dropped from warm to harder than a nail.

"No. No one tells me anything."

"Maighdeann-ròin Beatrice is due tomorrow."

The smile dropped from Ro's face in unison with Seraphina's stomach. "How long is she staying?"

"She's requested my presence for the entire summer, and you know I can't say no to that."

"No one says no to Beatrice," Ro said, her tone dark.

*Oh gods.* A whole summer with Beatrice?

"You can't run from her or your responsibilities, no matter how much you want to hide from it. You know that." Jack gazed out the glass windows, the crashing waves the only sound in the room for a few beats, his expression hard to read. "Doesn't matter, though. We'll still have fun. And I have today off."

Ro threw her arms around her brother and whooped. "You hear that, Fi? We'll be partying tonight!" She danced away, her hips swaying to a beat only she could hear.

*Oh boy.*

Ro and Jack's Merrow metabolism meant she could drink a lot more than Seraphina could. So far, Seraphina had avoided most of the partying at school, but that wouldn't be the case here. A fire on the beach could be fun, though.

"Well, let's make salt while the waves crash," Ro said as she danced out of the living room. She threw over her shoulder, "Coming, Fi?"

Ro didn't want her to swim. Her polite tone made that clear. "No, I can't keep up and it'll spoil your fun. Besides, it's been what, six months since you got to swim in your true form?" Ro nodded, her gaze assessing Seraphina in a way she'd been doing a lot lately. Like she judged Seraphina and found her wanting. "I'll just chill out in the library."

Making a face, Ro made a beeline for the stairs. "Your loss!"

Seraphina glanced back at Jack, who stood with his hands in his pockets, that look back on his face. She had a feeling she'd be seeing more of it the longer Beatrice stayed at the house. Beatrice did that, turned people hard and distant, much like Seraphina used to be around her grandfather.

A shiver slivered down her spine. One weekend with that woman had been enough to convince her she'd never want to spend any more time with her. What would a whole summer be like?

# 2

## A QUIET NIGHT IN

### (EAVESDROPPING NEVER PAID OFF)

A rustle of cloth announced Dorothy's presence in the library, followed by a click as light flooded the room. Seraphina glanced up from the wingback chair she'd curled up in.

"Excuse me, Miss Lastra, but would you be wanting any dinner? It's getting past time for me to leave for the night."

The mariner's clock chimed nine times as Seraphina pulled herself out of the book world and into this one. "Sorry, I got sucked into my book."

Dorothy's expression didn't change, but her fingers clenched the tea towel she held, and the faintest smell of salty air emanated off her.

It took all Seraphina's effort to keep the smile on her face. "Yes, I would like dinner, but I can make it." As soon as the words left her mouth, she knew made a mistake.

Dorothy's lips tightened, but her voice remained neutral as she said, "Nonsense. That is my role in this house, along with everything else. How does soup and a sandwich sound?"

"Excellent, thank you." The corners of Seraphina's lips wobbled with the strain of appearing friendly.

"It'll be ready in ten minutes in the dining room." With a sharp turn, Dorothy disappeared.

*Well, crap. That went swimmingly.*

The smile drained from Seraphina's face as she slumped back in the chair. Ro and Jack had left four hours ago, which wasn't a long time in the grand scheme of things, but she'd expected them back by now for food.

"Ugh." Seraphina smacked her forehead. They would've eaten any fresh kills they'd caught. She really should've set an alarm. Day one and already off to a poor start with Dorothy.

She twisted to stretch her back and was rewarded with a satisfying pop between her shoulder blades. As she walked by the shelves on her way out, she put the book back, leaving the library as pristine as she had found it. Too many years of leaving no trace wherever she lived had made the movement automatic.

Right before she passed the last set of books, something rattled behind her. She whirled, but just books met her glance. Shrugging, she turned around to leave, when something cold trickled down her spine. It felt as if a ghost breathed on her, the icy breeze slithering up and down as if it had a mind of its own. Her fingers curled into fists while she battled back the panic.

*No. Ghosts weren't real.*

Magic, Shapeshifters, Selkies, and Merrowmen were, but not ghosts. She was almost... certain. She left the room before she found out differently.

***

Music blared into Seraphina's ears, and she jolted awake, fumbling to shut it off before her ears bled. Peeling herself off her keyboard, she wiped the half-dried drool from her cheek, chuckling when her fingers found the imprint from the keys. She could type on her face. Ro would tease her for days if she knew.

Her smile faded as she checked the clock. It had been hours since she'd had dinner and come upstairs. Where was Ro?

Heaviness settled on Seraphina's shoulders. It was just like at school. They'd make plans to hang out, and Ro would forget. Or even worse, Seraphina suspected Ro blew her off on purpose.

But Ro hadn't seen her brother in a long time. What difference did it make if they didn't include her this time? They had all summer to hang out together. The same could not be said for Jack, who Ro only saw in small doses.

Without the music to fill it, the silence in the house was all-consuming, pressing down on her. Feeling lost and needing to move, Seraphina wandered down the hall to Ro's room.

Seraphina rapped lightly on the door. "Ro? Are you here?" When no response came, she pushed the door open. The light from the hall left a boxed pattern on the carpet. She peeked in and caught the outlines of Ro's untouched bed.

Of course, she wasn't here. Why would she be?

As she turned to go, she paused. Just because Ro hadn't come back to get her didn't mean she didn't want Seraphina to join her on the beach. And if this summer was anything like the last, there'd be a bonfire hidden in the dunes. If she could find the fire, maybe she'd find Ro and Jack. Or she'd find an entire group of people she didn't know.

Her foot tapped the ground.

First things first. She needed to find the party, and then she could decide if she'd venture out on her own. She crossed Ro's room and stepped out onto the damp surface of the balcony. Leaning over the railing, she peered in both directions, trying to see a flicker of light.

Below her, the patio door opened. Thinking it was Ro, she hung over the edge and almost called out when she heard the frosty tones of Dorothy. She eased herself off the railing and stepped back, trying to make as little noise as possible. With the crashing waves and the offshore breeze, Dorothy shouldn't know she was here, but she didn't want to take any chances.

"Why we must accommodate that girl is beyond me. She didn't even have the decency to check in about dinner. I had to go to her."

Seraphina cringed.

"Miss Roslynn likes her, Dot," the low timbered voice of Dannings said in response. "And we do what the boss says."

"Roslynn is not the boss of me."

"Not yet, anyway."

"Not until she is, Michael." Disapproval coated Dorothy's tone as if she'd been dipped in it.

Seraphina frowned. Ro didn't run the Griffiths' colony, Beatrice did, with an iron fist. Even if she didn't, Ro's mom would be next in line, wouldn't she?

"Is everything ready for the Maighdeann-ròin's arrival?" Dannings asked, obviously to appease Dorothy.

"Of course. Do you think I do not know my job?"

"Och, why are you in such a bad mood, Dot? You know I'm not accusing you of not doing your job properly."

"*You* aren't," Dorothy said in a voice tinged with bitterness.

"What does that mean?"

Dannings and Dorothy moved across the lawn, their voices growing fainter. "You know what that means. And that girl doesn't help matters."

"Leave off the human, Dot. She could be a lot worse, you know, running you ragged or causing mischief."

"That girl couldn't cause mischief if someone handed it to her on a plate."

Even though Dorothy wasn't wrong, Seraphina still grimaced. That could be her epitaph, especially this last year.

They walked into the path of the silvery light of the moon and stopped as Dorothy placed a hand on Dannings' arm. "Having the Maighdeann-ròin here for the entire summer brings ill tidings, Michael."

"Hush," Dannings said urgently, "They may hear you."

"I don't care if they do. That woman is up to something, you mark my words."

"Even if she is, it's for the good of the colony."

"You are so naïve. She does nothing that doesn't benefit her first and the colony second."

She leaned forward to hear more, eager to learn what Ro wouldn't tell her, but Dannings drew Dorothy away deeper into the shadows and Seraphina could only get snatches of the words spoken. Defeated, she stepped back inside.

It didn't matter. She wouldn't understand it and Ro wouldn't explain it. She'd end up right where she was, on the outside looking in. Just like what would happen if she crashed the bonfire party. Her stomach twisted at the thought.

Maybe she shouldn't have come.

Ro didn't seem to want her, and Dorothy definitely didn't. Add in the terrifying grandmother and it spelled nothing but disaster.

But would going home be any better?

## 3

### THE MORNING AFTER

(THE TIDE WAS OUT)

Absorbed in a video about fixing the binding on a book, Seraphina didn't hear Ro knock until Ro flopped on the bed and groaned. Seraphina took her headphones off, the woman's soothing voice from the video dropping to murmurs. She spun in her seat to find Ro sprawled across the bed, dark circles under her eyes.

"Ugh, I'm exhausted."

"Did you have fun last night?"

"We did. On our swim, we ran into the Watson brothers, and they invited us to their party. It was off the hook. Dylan danced with fire, which ended as expected. Him running into the sea to put himself out." Ro chuckled. "Idiot."

"Who is Dylan?"

"One of the guys who lives down the beach. I don't think you've met him. And then Jack challenged Nathanial to a drinking duel. And as his second, honor demanded I keep up." She massaged her forehead. "Although that last drink might have been one too many."

"Sounds like fun. When did you crawl in?" Seraphina asked around the lump in her throat. She'd promised herself she wouldn't be upset about Ro ditching her, but now that the moment had arrived, it was much harder to keep.

"Five." Ro sat up on her elbows. "Poor Jack had a meeting at nine. I only hope he made it, because otherwise, father will be pissed."

"He made it. I passed him on the stairs on my way back from a walk this morning. He looked like a zombie, but a functioning one." Seraphina kept her voice as level as she could. "I'm glad you had fun."

"What did you get up to?"

"Oh, the usual. Reading and researching college majors. Getting lost down the rabbit hole of what I want to be when I grow up."

"Fi, we've talked about this. Many, many times. You love books. Study English. Become a professor. Yada, yada, yada."

Ro's condescending tone grated on Seraphina's nerves. "I don't want to study English, Ro. I mean, I do, but not as a career. It's too... focused. Besides, getting a teaching position is more challenging than you make it sound." Bitterness crept into Seraphina's voice. "I'm not you. I don't have a family to fall back on if I fail."

"It's not all that and a bag of chips, Fi. Trust me. At least you have options."

"You have options, Ro. Don't say you don't." Seraphina waved at the house. "You can do whatever you want. Your family supports you in everything."

Ro barked out a laugh. "You have no idea what you're talking about. My *family* only supports what works in their favor."

The words mirrored what Dorothy had said the night before, but was that really the case? Not based on anything Seraphina had seen all the times she'd stayed with Ro's family. "That's not true."

"You're wrong, but whatever." Ro sat up on the edge of the bed. "All they care about is going to the right schools and meeting the right people."

"That's more than I have. I don't even know if my aunt cares if I go to college or not."

"I'm sure she does, Fi. You never bother to ask her about it."

Seraphina's head popped up. "What are you talking about? The last time we spoke, we talked about the weather, Ro. The weather. She couldn't wait to get off the phone."

"I'm not surprised."

Stung, Seraphina asked, "What's that supposed to mean?"

The space between them grew in the silence that fell, the churning of Seraphina's stomach mimicking the waves crashing on the shore outside her window. Emotions flowed across Ro's face, too many to catch, before she dropped eye contact and focused on her dangling feet.

A twinge of guilt cut through the churn. Ro never showed that much emotion.

Seraphina opened her mouth to ask her what was wrong when Ro said, "Nothing. Forget I said it." She dragged herself to her feet. "I'm ravenous, and you know how grouchy I get when hungry. I'm headed down for food. Wanna come?"

Seraphina wanted to join her, to smooth everything over, but the hurt of being left behind and that last comment wouldn't let her. "Nah, I'm good. I ate earlier."

"Okay. Well, I'd better hit it before Beatrice arrives."

"She's already here."

"What? When did she arrive?"

The panic on Ro's face surprised Seraphina. The controlled expression that followed immediately after did not.

"Around two, I think. I heard the car and peeked out the window."

Seraphina had studied Beatrice from behind the cotton sheer curtain when she'd arrived in casual blue slacks and a button-down shirt. Her long silver hair had been swept up at the back and she wore a brightly colored necklace, the blues and greens twinkling in the sun. It always surprised her that Beatrice looked like she could be anyone's grandmother. Until Beatrice pinned her with her gaze and stripped Seraphina down to the bone.

"Did she see you?"

"I don't know. Maybe." Seraphina shrugged. What difference did it make? She'd likely ignore her, anyway. "I'm not sure where she is right now, but the house has been quiet."

"Hopefully, that means she's resting. I thought I had more time." Ro straightened her shoulders, all remnants of the slouch and hangover gone, at least on the outside. "I'll catch you later, Fi. Dinner will be at seven sharp with proper attire."

*Oh gods.* She'd forgotten about the clothes. What she'd brought wouldn't be formal enough for dinner, let alone in the daytime. Seraphina watched her walk away. "Okay."

At the door, Ro paused. "We'll have fun this summer together, Fi, even with Beatrice here. I promise."

Seraphina nodded, but kept her lips pressed tight.

*Who was she trying to convince, herself or me?*

# 4

## THE CIRCLING SHARK

### (She Should've Chosen Something Else)

An hour later, the wind tugged on Seraphina's hair as she sat on a dune. She moved a strand that slashed across her face and stuck to her lips, hugging her knees tighter. After Ro had left, sitting still and staring at a screen became unbearable.

"What a mess."

She had no idea what had happened to their friendship, but if she didn't fix it this summer, her last year would be torture. Not only was she a pariah in school thanks to that stupid paper in Grindler's class, but even Ro was sick of her.

In May, she had dreaded asking Ro what she was doing for the summer, worried the response would be like spring break, nothing to do with her. When Ro mentioned the Hamptons and assumed Seraphina was coming with her, a little piece of the cold broken bits inside warmed up.

But the distance remained between them, rushing in and out like the tide. When it was good, it was good, but when it wasn't... Ro had mastered saying snarky comments that went deeper than their surface meaning, but she'd never aimed those comments at Seraphina before.

Until now.

Seraphina crunched the sand under her toes. Maybe she should go home. She could stay for the week, take a train and bus home from there. It'd be a hellish day, but wouldn't it be better than here, with a friend who sniped at her and a terrifying grandmother who ignored her existence?

The sharp tang of seaweed and salt assailed her, and she dropped her chin on her knees.

*No. Not yet.*

Her aunt wouldn't stop her from coming home, but she probably wouldn't welcome it either. Seraphina didn't blame her; the memories would be suffocating for them both. Her nails dug into her palms, the stinging pain keeping her grounded. She would've thought four years would have been enough time to take the edge off the memory of that day, but apparently not. Maybe it wouldn't be so bad here. It had to be better than home, right?

Her uncertainty said so much more about the state of their friendship than any comment ever could.

How did they get here?

"Ugh!" she said as she flopped back.

The sunlight flickered behind her closed eyelids, reminding her of the shapes of the trees through the window of her room at home. She couldn't escape it, no matter where she went. She sat up. Brooding on the beach wouldn't get her any answers, and she needed the bathroom, anyway. She stood and swiped her butt before wandering back to the house.

She used the thick grass to get rid of the last of the sand on her feet and then slipped into the living room. She could hear voices coming from the study at the back of the house and she veered away, crossing the hall to get to the stairs.

As she passed the library, she paused. There was still an hour or two before dinner and reading sounded so much better than staring at a screen. Her feet were already walking before she finished the thought.

Ro was right. She loved books, but she didn't know if she wanted to study them. It didn't feel like the right fit. Maybe it wasn't supposed to. She'd figure it out later. After she finished her book. And survived dinner. By the end of the summer, at the very least.

She pulled *Rebecca* off the shelf and curled up in her favorite leather armchair, the voices in her head quieting as she focused on the words.

An hour later, she closed the book, smiling as she smoothed her palm over the cover. With Beatrice in the house, she probably should have chosen a different book, but the ominous tone suited the upcoming dinner she needed to get ready for.

After putting *Rebecca* back in its spot, she skimmed the rest of the titles for a book to bring to her room in case she needed a retreat. As she moved to another shelf, a swirl of cold air moved up her spine to her shoulders. It felt almost personal.

As if it came from within.

*No.* It was her brain flavored by what she had just read. Gothic fiction was out. She needed something light to combat the heaviness. Her fingers skipped past *The Castle of Otranto* and settled on *A Room with a View.* She'd always meant to read it after watching the movie and it had no horror elements in it. She bent over to grab it. Before she knew what was happening, she pulled out a different book as if it had stuck to her fingers.

She read the title and grimaced. She'd rather read *The Grapes of Wrath* again, which she loathed, then a book on fables. When she tried to slide the book back in its slot, it wouldn't go in, as if resisting her attempts.

*Weird.*

Even in the Magic Community, inanimate objects remained inanimate and didn't resist being re-shelved. Maybe something blocked it. She stuck her fingers in the gap and felt around, but found nothing. As she pulled her hand away, the icy feeling traveled down her arms. Her fingers grazed an old leather spine and the book it belonged to jumped into her hand. Heart pounding, she read the title, *The Manual of Etiquette.*

Her eyes flicked from side to side, looking for the joke or the person pulling the prank, but there was nowhere to hide in the library.

*What the heck was going on?*

"I see you've found a book to read," a haughty voice said from the doorway.

Seraphina jumped and stared wild-eyed at Ro's big, bad grandmother.

Beatrice's eyes narrowed for a fraction of a second, as if sizing Seraphina up for the first time instead of seeing her as an annoying gnat to swat away.

Swallowing hard, Seraphina replied, "Um, yes. Hello, Mrs. Griffiths."

"Seraphina Lastra, is it not? One of Roslynn's friends from school?"

"Yes, ma'am. Her roommate."

"Ah. I remember now. The human girl born of Shapeshifter parents." Beatrice stepped out of the doorway and moved closer, circling behind Seraphina.

"Yes, ma'am."

"How long are you going to be our guest?" The tips of Beatrice's canines peeked through from behind her bloodless lips as she circled ever closer.

"Ro invited me to stay for the summer, but I may head home."

Beatrice moved around again, causing Seraphina to shiver as the chilly feeling retracted to hover near her heart. "You mean Roslynn, my granddaughter?"

"Yes, ma'am." A warm buzz filled Seraphina's head, the conflict between it and the cold near the center of her body discombobulating her.

"Wasn't that nice of her." Sarcasm laced Beatrice's words.

Seraphina winced and then worked it into a polite smile that probably looked more like constipation than friendliness, but it was the best she could do.

Something in her face caught Beatrice's attention. She stopped moving and leaned in, her eyes scanning Seraphina. After a moment where Seraphina tried not to breathe, Beatrice stepped back and played with the sea glass necklace around her neck. "Please, stay for the duration, if that is what you agreed to do."

Seraphina blinked, feeling more weight to the words than they appeared to have. "Of course."

"You've already made good use of the library, something that granddaughter of mine fails to do. I wonder if she'll ever apply herself appropriately, especially since she left her guest," the words snapped out of her mouth as if practicing elocution, "to fend for herself."

Beatrice's feet moved again as she circled around Seraphina.

The pounding of her heart sounded loud to Seraphina's ears, but she didn't want Ro to get in trouble. "Ro, um, Roslynn had a few things to take care of," Seraphina lied. "She asked me to come, but I wanted to read. I really like to read."

"Yes, you would, wouldn't you?"

Seraphina didn't know what to say to that, so she remained quiet. It had always worked with her grandfather, who had soon gotten bored and dismissed her. Thick silence fell between them as the air grew strong with the smell of brine.

The smell overwhelmed her as Beatrice continued to walk around her. Feeling like a seal targeted for dinner by a shark, Seraphina blurted out. "Yes."

Beatrice moved closer until she stood in front of her.

*Oh gods.*

"May I?" She held out her hand for the books Seraphina clutched to her chest.

"Of course."

"Interesting choice of reading. Classic, but not in the gaudy human sense. More substance, fewer scales."

Seraphina clamped her lips shut, so that she didn't rise to the bait.

Beatrice flipped through the books, pausing on some pages longer than others. Closing the books with a snap that made Seraphina twitch, Beatrice handed the books back. "Read whatever you like, Seraphina. And if there are any books you'd like to keep, set them to one side. At the end of the summer, I will see what your choices are. If they are books I am willing to part with, you may keep them."

"That is very good of you, Mrs. Griffiths, but I couldn't possibly take any of your books."

"Beatrice, please. And you will do as you're told."

A shiver ran down Seraphina's spine at the implied threat if she didn't.

"They are mine to give away. Put the books you want on that table, and I will instruct the servants to leave them be."

"Of course. Thank you."

Beatrice's lips curled up, a full set of teeth on display. "You are welcome. Dinner is in an hour and a half. Do be on time." She pivoted on her heel and left the library.

Seraphina sank into the chair, her heart pounding as if she'd run a mile. No one could do scary like Beatrice. Not even her grandfather.

# 5

## PRE-DINNER HIJINKS

### (SHE WASN'T PREPARED FOR THIS)

Seraphina laid out the only formal dress she'd brought with her. She could dress it up with a half pink jacket, but it only changed it from summer wear to appropriate for a chilly coffee shop. Sighing, she walked over to Ro's room to see if she could borrow a few dresses.

At her knock, Ro yelled, "Come in."

"Hey."

"Hey," Ro called from her walk-in closet.

"What's all this?" Seraphina asked, eyeing a mound of dresses covering Ro's bed.

"Choice," Ro said as she emerged with another armful of clothes dressed in a bathrobe and her hair wrapped in a towel. She dumped the dresses on the bed, took a step back, and then grabbed a leather strapless dress off the pile and took it back into the closet.

Seraphina played with her lip and approached the clothes problem from another angle. Ro had never said no, but it still bugged Seraphina to ask. Her aunt had put money in her account, but it only covered the basics, and Seraphina didn't like to push for more. The less she asked for, the more likely she'd receive it. And she had no idea how much money her aunt had to give, anyway.

"I ran into your grandmother in the library earlier," she finally said.

"Oh, how did it go?"

"Well, she's just as scary as I remember, but she told me to set aside any books I wanted, and she'd let me take a few. It was weird." A shiver ran through her as she remembered the books she pulled out with no desire to read them. And that weird cold sensation that preceded it. "It was almost as if I had no choice."

"If Beatrice told you to take the books, you have to take them."

"Yeah, she said something similar when I mentioned maybe going home."

The rustling in the closet stopped for a moment, and then a hanger screeched along the rod. Seraphina had no idea what she was searching for. She already had at least half a dozen dresses on the bed.

"Is that what you want, to go home?" Ro said from the depths of the closet.

"I don't know. Not really. But..."

"Beatrice."

"Exactly." Seraphina crossed her arms as if to ward off a chill, "And home is... fraught, I guess would be the right word. I can't avoid it forever, but I'll put it off as long as I can."

Ro came back out of the closet, a single floor length dress in her hand. "I'm sorry she's going to be here. I know I promised she wouldn't, but you can't tell my grandmother what to do."

"I kind of got that impression the first time I met her when she told the president of the school to go away, and he did."

Ro smirked. "That was one of those moments where I actually liked Beatrice. Mr. Barnaby is a petty little toad."

Seraphina fiddled with the fray on her jean shorts. "Speaking of being liked, I don't have the right clothes for formal dinners with Beatrice. I wondered if I could borrow one or two things."

She held her breath while Ro slipped the dress on.

"I figured. All the dresses on the bed are for you to use while you're here. Take the ones you want. If you don't like them, we can find something else. Manaan knows, I own tons of clothes I never wear. It's like they breed in my closet."

Seraphina laughed, relief making her sag. "Or it could be all the shopping you do."

"That too." Ro spun around and gestured. "What do you think? Conservative enough for the old battle ax?"

The dress had buttons down the front and a full skirt in an iridescent material. It had fluttery sleeves that moved as she gestured.

"Definitely. It's gorgeous, Ro, and it really sets off your eyes."

Ro's unmasked eyes swirled in the colors of the ocean depths. When her emotions ran high, they were a deep blue, almost black. Right now, turquoise with hints of darker greens triumphed. It was one thing Seraphina envied. That, and her metabolism. And her confidence. If only she could be more like Ro, everything would be easier.

"Well, I don't know about that, but there you go." Ro frowned at Seraphina and then said, "You'd better get a move on. Grab as many as you can carry and get ready. We can't do anything about the shoes, but hopefully Beatrice won't notice."

Glancing down at her Converse low tops, Seraphina said, "I've brought a few pairs of sandals. They should work well enough."

Unwrapping her towel, Ro sat at the vanity table. She applied eyeshadow to her lids and then cocked her head at Seraphina. "What are you waiting for? You don't want to be late."

"Good point." Seraphina scooped up a pile of dresses and went back to her room to get dressed. "I'll knock when I'm done."

"Okay."

Seraphina wrestled with the door and only hoped she didn't have to wrestle with Beatrice at the table. Gods knew she'd lose.

***

At exactly ten to seven, Seraphina knocked on Ro's door.

Ro answered it, her makeup flawless and her short black hair set in wavy curls. She gave Seraphina a quick glance and said, "That'll do, Fi."

"I hope so."

They headed down the hall for the stairs.

"Remember, you don't sit until she does and when she's finished with a course, so are you."

"Right." Seraphina's nerves stretched taut, hoping she didn't create a faux pas that caused drama for Ro.

They joined the rest of the family in the living room. Ro's mom, Rowena, lounged on a chair with a martini. Jefferson, Ro's dad, stood at the bar making drinks as Jack discussed a business deal with them.

"There you two are, right on time," Rowena said, rising to give Ro and Seraphina a peck on their cheeks.

"Hello, Mother."

Jefferson glanced over his shoulder and said, "I'm making you both cucumber martinis, alright?"

"Thanks, Dad."

"Thanks, Mr. Griffiths."

Jack chuckled as Jefferson turned around and muttered, "Jefferson or Jeff. Mr. Griffiths is Rowena's father. May he rest in tides and sunlight."

"Sorry," Seraphina said, a flush heating her cheeks.

"How's school going, girls?" Jefferson asked, his attention back to the cocktails in front of him.

"Fine. I still don't know what I'm doing there. All we learn is stuff that isn't useful," Ro said as she accepted her glass from her dad.

Seraphina glanced at Ro in surprise, a small frisson of alarm rushing through her. She thought Ro liked their boarding school.

"You know why, Roslynn. Stop asking to be transferred, especially since it's your last year," Rowena said. "It's an excellent school and you'll meet all the right people."

"Who? Stupid humans and potential business partners for dad. Just the people I want to be around." Ro rolled her eyes.

"Roslynn." Her mother warned with a glance in Seraphina's direction.

With a sheepish glance at Seraphina, Ro said, "Sorry, Fi. You're exempt from that."

Taking a sip from her drink to hide her expression, Seraphina shrugged a shoulder. She liked the school for that reason. All the humans around her made her feel less like an outsider. Until this past year where she'd proved that feeling wrong.

"You are being rude to the guest you invited, Roslynn," Beatrice announced from the door. Like a tableau, they all faced her,

Rowena rising from the couch and Jack's face tightening. "And what have you done to your hair?"

Ro crossed the room and gave her grandmother a polite peck on the cheek. "I cut it short. It makes it easier to get to class on time. They're super early."

"It is an abomination. I expect you to grow it out again."

A collective hush filled the room as the seconds stretched into minutes. Seraphina flicked a glance at Ro but couldn't see her face.

"Yes, grandmother," Ro finally said, the words leached of all tone.

"Mother, this is Roslynn's friend– "

"We have already met," Beatrice said, cutting Rowena off. She turned her autocratic eye at Seraphina. "Did you set aside any books like I told you to?"

Seraphina swallowed and said, "Yes, thank you. You have a wonderful library."

"I am aware."

Jefferson made a movement that he checked, shoving his hands in his pockets.

"What, Jefferson? They are my books and if I wish to give them away, I will."

"Of course, Beatrice," he said, the words strangled in his throat.

"Shall we go in?"

"Of course, Mother," Rowena said as she set her cocktail down. Jefferson rushed to take her arm and guide her across the room, while Jack paused before Seraphina and cocked his elbow.

"Shall we?"

Seraphina put her drink down and nodded, placing her hand on the inside of his arm like she'd seen Ro do once with her father.

Ro followed her grandmother out, and they filed into the dining room. If it wasn't so tense, Seraphina would've enjoyed it. It felt like a Jane Austen novel. Except that Beatrice was Lady Catherine de Bourgh in this scenario. Stiff, haughty, and very judgmental.

Dinner was going to be a treat.

**6**

—  ·  —

# FORMALITY AT ITS WORST

### (THE FOOD WASN'T THE ONLY THING THAT SUCKED)

They filed around the table and stood in front of their chairs. Beatrice looked at them over her nose and then sat down, Dorothy helping to push the tall chair in. Seraphina waited until the others moved, but Jefferson and Jack both looked at her expectantly.

Flushing again, she sat, and then they sat as well. Maybe she should've read that etiquette book. If the whole summer was going to be like this, she might need to. Dorothy rushed around the table, placing the first course, a soup, and filling up wine glasses.

The crystal sparkled in the chandelier's light, like the sun after a hard frost. A shiver traveled down Seraphina's spine, and she clenched her hands together to stop it from showing. She was out of practice, but then showing no reaction wasn't a thing she had needed to do at school.

No one said anything until Beatrice took her first taste of the soup. When she put her spoon in it again and raised it to her lips, everyone else picked up their spoons and ate as well. Seraphina scooped a small amount of soup and sipped it.

*Oh gods.* Of course, it'd be seafood.

Ro glanced at her. Seraphina gave a tight smile and took another mouthful, trying not to gag as the cold broth hit the back of her throat. She swallowed the soup as quick as possible to avoid the taste lingering in her mouth. Her only hope was that Beatrice ate fast, so she wouldn't have to eat too much of it. She hated seafood.

Last summer, Dorothy had made her separate meals when they hadn't eaten out. Guess that didn't apply for family dinners.

After three more gulps, Beatrice set her spoon down and everyone else followed, even if the spoon was halfway to their mouths. Seraphina said a silent thanks and did the same.

Dorothy removed the course and brought the next one in. Thankfully, a salad. She could survive on salad.

After the last dish had been placed, Beatrice picked up her fork and took a bite. "Excellent, Dorothy."

Dorothy nodded, a gleam in her eye the only sign she'd even heard the compliment.

That signaled yet another clattering of silverware as they dove into their salads. The acidic taste of seaweed filled Seraphina's mouth and she almost spit it out. It took every skill she possessed to keep her face as neutral as possible. Across the table, Ro tucked her lips in to stop a smile.

Why was Ro enjoying this?

Seraphina swallowed the bite almost whole and then lingered over scooping up the next one. The rest of them had a few bites left by the time Seraphina lifted her fourth mouthful.

"You don't like the salad, Seraphina?" Beatrice asked.

"It's good, but I want to save room for the rest of the courses."

Beatrice raised one eyebrow and then turned her gaze on Ro. "You would do well to learn from Seraphina, Roslynn. You can't keep shoveling it in and expect it to not show."

Seraphina's eyes widened as Ro stopped her fork in midair, along with everyone else at the table. "I swam for six hours yesterday, grandmother. I need to refuel."

"Dorothy's already told me you ate enough for four people this afternoon."

Ro finished chewing and took a sip of wine before responding. "That was good of her."

"It's her job, Roslynn."

"Then she's doing it well."

Beatrice's expression could melt sand into glass, but Ro kept eating.

"Did you catch anything?" Beatrice asked, the tone neutral but the undercurrent clear.

"I did, but Roslynn didn't want to stop, so she swam while I did," Jack said.

"I didn't ask you, Jackson. I asked your sister," Beatrice snapped. Ro opened her mouth, but Beatrice waved it away. "No matter. What do you plan to do while you are here?"

Ro set down her fork and blotted her mouth with her napkin. "We thought we'd spend time at the beach and get my driver's license."

"Why would you need to do that? Dannings can drive you wherever you wish to go."

"To fit in, Beatrice. Everyone's learning at school. Some are even driving back after the summer." Ro paused. "You don't want me to stand out, do you?"

Brine and salt washed over the dining room, making it hard for Seraphina to taste anything. In any other given moment, that would be a good thing, but not tonight. The last meal they'd had with Beatrice wasn't this bad. Not even close. Normally, Ro gave her one-word answers, prompting Beatrice to move on. Why was she challenging her?

Seraphina flicked a glance around the table without moving her head to avoid attracting attention. Jack's jaw clenched, his discomfort clear. Rowena and Jefferson finished the last bites on their plate like automatons, no expressions, just scooping and chewing.

Dorothy stood behind Ro, a small smile on her face. When Seraphina met her gaze, she lifted her chin, her opinion clear.

Seraphina dropped her gaze and played with the last of the seaweed on her plate.

"Very well." Beatrice's voice broke through the wall of silence as if breaking through the surface tension of the ocean. "It will be good use of your and Seraphina's time, since you won't spend it improving your mind."

Ro's lips tightened.

The fork slipped from Seraphina's fingers and clattered to the plate. Heat rushed up her cheeks.

"Is that a problem, Seraphina?"

*Keep it simple, Seraphina.*

"No, it's not a problem," Seraphina spray painted a polite smile on her face. "Thank you for including me."

"Of course, dear. Any friend of Roslynn's is a friend of ours."

Rowena choked on her salad and took a quick sip of wine to clear it.

"Is that not so, Rowena?" Beatrice challenged.

"Yes, mother."

The longer Seraphina sat at the dinner table, the more she understood why Ro came back from visits with Beatrice a hardened shell of the girl who left. Seraphina would take her grand-father any day over this icy queen who threw daggers with every remark.

Dorothy cleared the salad plates, and the next course arrived, a small filet of white fish, with a lemony sauce and asparagus stacked next to it.

*Oh gods, she was going to starve.*

Beatrice picked up her knife and fork and cut into the fish, saying before it reached her mouth, "Jackson, you will teach them."

Jefferson frowned and set his wineglass down. "Jackson is in the middle of an important deal, Beatrice. He can't spend hours away teaching the girls how to drive."

Jack's movements stilled next to her, but his fingers tightened on his knife.

"Nonsense. He only needs a few hours with them. He can easily spare the time. After all, did he do any work in the past two days?"

Jefferson's mouth tightened. "He's been working seven days a week for the past eight months. I gave him leeway to spend time with his sister."

Beatrice raised her eyebrows. "How generous of you."

Seraphina glanced up at Ro, who stared at her plate. *Jeezus, when would this meal end?*

"It was, Beatrice, extremely generous and I am grateful to father for providing it to me. I did, however, spend the morning finalizing a memorandum after a conference call," Jack said, his voice controlled.

"Of course you did, dear boy. You know which side your fish is battered on." She pressed her lips together and then cut into her fish. "I do not see any issues with Jackson taking a few hours out of his day to do this one small thing I am asking of him. Do you, Rowena?"

"No, mother, but only if he limits it to two hours a day," Rowena said, her mouth in a tight line.

"Excellent. The matter is solved then."

The family dynamics at the table suffocated Seraphina. It felt as if they were walking on a tightrope and expected the rope to fail at any moment. She thought briefly to her comfortable dorm room, with the window seat and large tub. She'd give anything to be there right now, even among the construction.

Anything would be better than this.

# 7

## SNEAKING OUT

### (Looping and Laughing)

The minty freshness of mouthwash overwhelmed Seraphina's senses as she gargled the fish taste away in the attached bathroom of her room. Maybe she could pick up snacks and hide them in the room to compensate for the dinners.

No. Dorothy would find them and apparently report on her. If nothing else, she'd learned something tonight at dinner. Don't trust the servants.

The rest of dinner had been less painful than the first part, thanks to business talk. Beatrice peppered Jack and Jefferson about the deal they worked on while they ate their way through one more fish dish and then a tart baked apple for dessert. Beatrice spoiled it by only taking a few bites. From here on out, Seraphina planned on gulping her dessert down as quick as she could.

After dinner, Beatrice ensconced herself in the study and called the family in one at a time. Ro went first. Luckily, Seraphina didn't appear on that list, so she escaped to her room to breathe easy.

A tap at her door had her spitting the mouthwash out. She wiped her mouth and yelled, "Come in!"

Ro wandered in wearing a tank top and shorts, her feet bare, carrying a bottle of wine with the cork sticking out. "Hey," she said as she closed the door. Her face scrunched up as she took in the old Harriman's Herbs t-shirt and pajama bottoms Seraphina wore. "What are you doing?"

"Getting ready for bed."

"Nuh uh. Get dressed, we're out of here."

Seraphina blinked at her. "Where are we going?"

"Bonfire at the beach." Ro wandered over to the window. "Crappy view of the drive. I wonder if she'll move you now," she murmured.

"What?" Seraphina asked as she rummaged in her drawers for a clean tank and pair of shorts.

"Nothing. Come on. Clock's ticking."

Her voice muffled by the shirt she pulled over her head, Seraphina asked, "What's the rush?"

"We only have a few hours before Beatrice notices."

Seraphina pulled her shorts on. "We're sneaking out?"

"Duh."

"Why?"

"Because Beatrice wants you in the house before she sets the alarm at 2 am and the rest of us go on our snàmh oidhche. If we tell her we're leaving, she'll set it earlier, just to spite us." Ro pulled Seraphina out of the bedroom and down the hall to an empty guest room with a view of the water.

The dark room mirrored hers, except it had a balcony and a much better view of the ocean. Ro's comment took on more meaning.

"Wait, did they give me the drive view because of who I am?"

Ro slid the patio doors open, Seraphina hot on her heels. "Who knows? That's Dorothy's job." She passed Seraphina the wine as she closed the patio doors behind them.

*Of course it was.* Seraphina walked to the edge and glanced down. The two-story drop loomed below her, the moon bathing the grass a silvery gray color. "Uh, how are we getting down?"

Ro took the wine bottle back and shoved it in her tight tank top between her boobs. "How do you think?" She climbed over the railing and crouched down, her hands sliding down the metal rods holding the top railing in place. A muffled thud showed she'd let go.

This was not Seraphina's idea of a good time. In fact, she'd rather be in her room reading than anywhere else right now.

"Fi," Ro hissed, "Come on."

Shaking her head, Seraphina followed Ro's movements over the balcony and let go. Her feet stung as she landed and then fell backward.

Ro had already moved halfway across the lawn, avoiding the patches of light blazing from the windows of the house.

Seraphina stood, wincing, and followed her. She slipped through the open gate to the stairs leading down from the grass to the water, careful not to bump it in case it squeaked.

Ro ran away from the house to find a spot to sit that wouldn't be seen if anyone looked out the windows. She plopped down and yanked the cork out of the wine, taking a deep drink.

Seraphina sat next to her and took a sip from the bottle as Ro handed it to her. She really didn't want to drink it, having not had enough food to soak up the alcohol. But she'd learned to go with it. Ro would gulp it down, anyway.

"Ro," she whispered. "Are you okay?"

"I don't want to talk about it."

Ro didn't want to talk about a lot recently. "Okay."

"What?"

Seraphina's stomach grumbled, and she blurted out, "Are we having fish for every meal?" before she could stop herself.

A lone laugh escaped, the tail end trailing away in the darkness. "Only when we eat with Beatrice."

The moon shimmered on the water. "How much will that be?"

"I don't know," Ro snapped as she laid back.

Seraphina bit back the response on the tip of her tongue and focused on the sound of the waves as they crashed on the beach.

Ro sighed, "Sorry. Beatrice makes me nuts. Mom and dad will eat at the club more now that Beatrice is here, which means fewer formal dinners. It'll probably be once a week or so."

"I can manage that," Seraphina said, her tone as neutral as possible.

"Manaan, she is such a bitch!" Ro sat up and hugged her knees. "She waltzes in and destroys everything."

"I take it your conversation was less fun than dinner, then?"

A bitter laugh escaped Ro. "That was a cakewalk compared to some dinners we've had. You have no idea what she's like."

"I have some idea, but not the same intensity as you." Seraphina frowned. "Did I get you in trouble by being in the library?"

"No. You could get me in trouble just by breathing. Don't worry about her. I can handle it."

"I don't want you to handle it if I'm causing it."

"Don't you?"

"What does that mean?" Seraphina's breath caught in her throat as she faced Ro.

Ro stared out at the water, her lips pressed together, not seeming to care as the emotions tightened across Seraphina's chest.

*What had happened to them?*

A sharp whistle pierced the air, breaking the building silence. Further down the shoreline, a figure wandered on the hard-packed sand.

Ro stood and sauntered toward them without saying a word.

Seraphina didn't move. She wasn't even sure what she was doing here. Fear that Ro only kept her around as a pity project rolled through Seraphina quicker than the water rolling toward the beach. Since the disaster in Grindler's class, more people had avoided her, but Ro hadn't. They simply had hung out less because of the classes they took.

*You idiot.* Ro was trying to shake her loose, and Seraphina hung on like the aftertaste of dinner. She pulled her knees closer to her and stared at the crashing waves, tears spilling down her cheeks.

The ocean roared as a lone seagull screamed overhead. She'd never seen one out this late. It must've lost its mate. Seraphina buried her toes deeper in the cool sand, feeling much the same way.

"Fi, come on!" Ro yelled, her voice carrying on the wind.

Seraphina glanced over at her. Ro stood midway between the figure near the water and Seraphina, her hand on her hip. "Well?"

The sadness eased. If Ro hadn't of wanted to hang out, she would've run ahead and left Seraphina behind. Seraphina stood and wiped the tears off her face before jogging to catch up.

As they neared, she heard Ro scream, "Simon!" and then throw herself at him.

Seraphina picked up the pace. The only thing she knew about Simon was his name. Ro had casually mentioned him after she'd come back from spring break, but Seraphina hadn't been fooled. It was the first time a boy's name crossed Ro's lips without sarcasm.

Ro hugged him and then slipped her hand into his.

Simon held out his hand. "Hi, I'm Simon."

"Seraphina," she said as she shook it.

He gave her an odd look and then glanced at Ro, who said, "She's cool. She knows."

Simon's eyes darted back to Seraphina's, and his hesitation became clear. "My parents were Shifters. My aunt's a Wielder. You can be yourself."

"Oh." Simon's mouth closed with a snap, followed by a frown. "Wait, how is any of that possible?"

"I have no idea."

He jerked his head back the way he came. "The party's down this way."

"Works for me," Ro said. "The farther we get from the house, the better."

Simon nudged Ro with his shoulder, but she just shrugged. He frowned and then turned to Seraphina. "So, your parents are both Shifters."

"Were. They died four years ago."

"I'm sorry."

"It's fine." It wasn't, but no one really wanted to know that. Mentioning that her parents were dead, either in the Magical Community or the human world, always ended the same way, with awkward silence.

"How is your aunt a Wielder then? Are you adopted?"

"No. My Uncle Patrick, also a Shifter, partnered outside his phylum."

Simon whistled. "I didn't think that was allowed."

"They made it happen." She wrapped her arms around herself and watched the water rush over her feet. Of all the people she had lost that day, she missed him the most.

"Are your parents from around here, then?"

"No. We go to school together, but her family's in Merricott," Ro said.

"Is that the Community in New Hampshire?"

"Yes."

"Cool. You're at the human school too?"

Seraphina glanced at Ro, who obviously hadn't told the boy she'd been talking to for three months anything about her. The gulf between them widened. "Well, I am human and it's a human boarding school, so..."

"Oh yeah. That makes sense," Simon mumbled as Ro laughed.

Ro loved tripping Community members up with Seraphina's background and how they knew each other. It wasn't common for MC folk to attend schools for humans, but all Ro's family had done so. Tradition was Ro's response to anyone asking from either community why she attended Harborwood.

There had to be more to it than that, but any time Seraphina had asked, Ro had shut her down, so she stopped trying. If Ro wanted her to know, she'd tell her.

Maybe.

Seraphina trailed behind them as they cut in across the sand to join a group of Merrowfolk, their human faces slipping the more they drank. There must be a ward set up by a local Wielder to warn them of non-MC people approaching. Maybe it'd go off, and they'd all scatter like crabs at sunset.

She doubted it, though. Seraphina never seemed to set off wards meant to keep her kind away, so she didn't expect it to be any different here.

However, that didn't stop the group from panicking at the sight of her. As they drew nearer, a few on the outer edge slid their human faces into place, the color draining out of their eyes.

She rolled her eyes. *Here we go again.* "Hey."

"Uh, what gives, White?" The taller of the two boys facing them had shifted his body to hide the group behind him.

"She's cool, Jones," Simon said.

Jones cocked his head at her. "You're human, though, right?"

Feeling like the night was on a loop, she sighed. "Yes. My parents were Shifters."

"Were you adopted?" The shorter of the two boys croaked out, his voice breaking midway through. Jones punched him in the arm.

"No."

"How does that happen?"

"No idea."

"Huh. Cool. Well, there's beer and pizza. Help yourself," the shorter guy said, waving his arm in the direction behind him. Everyone remained still, as if waiting for something to happen, so Seraphina didn't move. A log dropped off the top of the bonfire and rolled in a spray of sparks, which caused the short guy to say, "Hey Grif."

The air had a quality like what had happened at dinner, but worse. She glanced at Ro and a funny expression crossed her face. Something between wistful and hard, before a smile tugged at her lips.

"Jones, Samson," Ro said. "Still as dorky as ever, I see."

Jones' shoulders dropped as Samson asked, "Yeah, so? You're going to drink our beer anyway, right?"

"Absolutely. If you have enough."

"We do," Samson said.

"Excellent."

Whatever spell had been holding everyone stiff broke as Simon fist-bumped Jones. Conversation picked up again and Seraphina slipped through the crowds to find the pizza before they'd eaten it all. If they were anything like Ro, it'd be gone before the box lid closed.

**8**

# BONFIRE AT THE BEACH

## (Maybe It Would Be Alright)

A while later, Seraphina had her back against a dead tree, the sand warm under her feet as the fire crackled before her. A warm beer sat next to her. She'd only picked it up to fit in, not that it made any difference. After the usual banter of how she came to be, most of the crew went back to talking to each other.

Not that they were unfriendly, but they'd known each other far longer than her. After one patient girl explained all the connections, which totally confused her, Seraphina gave up and left them to it. Besides, she enjoyed watching the fire.

Ro wandered to the edges of the group, never far from Simon. When Seraphina lost sight of her on the other side of the bonfire, her large throaty laugh eased the tension that came with the thought Ro had left her here on her own.

She could handle being alone, but she had no idea how to get back into the house. Ro must've had a plan, though she usually did.

Ro plopped down next to her and held up her beer. Seraphina clinked it with her own and then took a drink, the bubbles fizzing on her tongue.

"Having fun?"

"Of course. Everyone's really nice."

A harsh laugh exploded from Ro, and she shook her head. "Nah, they aren't, but they don't know enough about you to be mean."

Seraphina's eyebrows rose. "Are they really like that?"

"Take Harborwood Academy and times it by 1000 and you'll get what this crew is about. They've been at it longer and it takes a while to warm up, especially for new girls."

"I'll be alright. I've figured out the art of the neutral face," Seraphina said, unease creeping back in.

Ro spit out her drink as she laughed. "No, you haven't."

"I have too!"

"No, Fi, you haven't. It's why they still pick on you at school. They only mess with people to get a reaction and you give it to them every time."

Seraphina scowled. "Well, they're a bunch of assholes, anyway."

"They're almost in our rearview mirror."

"Yep. College, here we come and a new bunch of assholes to deal with." The bitter aftertaste of the beer mirrored her tone.

"Nah, it'll be different." Ro said, her eyes shining in the flickering fire. "More people, more diversity. And much better food choices."

"You really don't like our school, do you?"

"No. I don't." Ro's fingers picked at the label on her beer. "But I didn't get a choice." She took a swift drink.

"Neither did I. I'm glad they sent you there, even if you aren't."

Ro bumped her shoulder with her own. "It's not all bad. It's mostly bad. Like 95% bad."

"Ro!" Seraphina said through her laughter.

"What? You know it's true. You can't possibly love the mystery casseroles they serve us, or the old grotty classrooms, or," Ro shuddered, "learning Latin."

"No, I don't, but the desserts are nice. And Latin could come in handy later."

"When? When are we going to need it?"

"You're planning on studying science, right?" Sarcasm dripped from Seraphina's words, and Ro rolled her eyes. "Aren't species' names based on Latin?"

"Fine. You have a point. But the food sucks."

"I finally won a point against the great Roslynn Griffiths." Seraphina punched the air with her fist.

"Shut up."

Two cold beer bottles appeared next to Seraphina's head, filling the space between them.

"Thought you'd be out by now, you lush," Simon said from above them.

Ro threw back the rest of her beer and grabbed the fresh one. "I wasn't, but I am now." They stared at each other so deeply that Seraphina could feel it, like the heat from the fire.

Simon nodded and then wandered back over to the main cluster of boys. Ro's mask dropped for a moment, and she looked at him like Seraphina looked at an ice cream sundae, but more intense than that, as if it was the last sundae on earth.

A lump filled her throat. "Soooooo, Simon then."

"Shut up."

"No, can't now that I've met him. He puts Matthew Corning to shame."

Ro sputtered through the beer she just swallowed. "I never liked Matthew Corning."

"Are you freaking kidding me? You drew his name in hearts, Ro, all over your philosophy notes."

"I did not."

"Did too." Seraphina grinned. "Remember, I borrowed them to make up for the class I missed? They were everywhere." She clasped her hands and fluttered her eyelashes at Ro. "He's so dreamy, Fi."

"I never said that!" Ro protested through her laughter.

"No, but you thought it. I know you did."

Ro pushed her over into the sand. "You're not going to let me forget it, are you?"

Seraphina sat back up. "No."

They lapsed back into a comfortable silence, the crack of the fire and the roar of the water interspersed with conversation and laughter.

She was going to miss this.

A loud argument broke out on the other side of the fire. A smile slid across Ro's face as she tilted her head to hear, but she didn't move.

"You don't have to keep me company, Ro. Go join them if you want."

Ro glanced at Seraphina, her eyes the blue of the deep. "Have you ever thought that perhaps I like the company I'm with? That I choose to be here?"

Seraphina blinked. Keeping her tone light, she said, "Yep, and I dismissed you as a crackpot."

"Then that makes two of us."

The tension in Seraphina melted away as she sat next to her best friend on the beach around a fire, like they had planned.

Maybe everything really would be alright.

# 9

## CARS AND CAFES

### (THE STING OF THE BACKLASH)

Two weeks later, Seraphina had just pulled on her favorite cut-off jean shorts and a simple tank top when she heard a knock. Her fingers trembled as she laced up her Converse sneakers.

Ro stuck her head in and asked, "Are you ready yet?"

Since the bonfire, it had almost been like old times. Tension still cropped up between them and Ro sometimes made a snarky crack, but it didn't feel like it had when they had first arrived. They filled the days with sunbathing, reading, a few parties, and driving lessons.

Another of which was imminent. The first five hadn't gone too bad, but Jack had insisted they learn on a manual transmission, which created a whole new level of anxiety. In his words, "You could drive anything if you learn on a stick first."

She had enough trouble paying attention to the road, the rearview mirror, and her speed. Adding shifting into another gear or remembering to put the clutch in when she stopped made it impossible.

Her cheeks burned when she remembered the first time she stalled the car at a busy traffic light, horns filling the air as Ro chortled in the back seat. Only Jack had remained calm, giving her instructions and telling her to ignore everyone.

"Yes. I think so."

"Ok. Meet you downstairs." Ro shut the door with a click.

Ro had taken to driving like it was her job. She had no issues with shifting, stopping, and playing with the radio at the same time. If Seraphina didn't know better, she'd think Ro had been driving for a while.

Or Seraphina was particularly inept.

It could go either way. She grabbed her purse and checked to make sure she had her learner's permit. She couldn't stall much longer, or they'd leave without her, and she'd never get her license. With a sigh, she headed downstairs.

Ro and Jack stood next to the twenty-year-old green Audi they'd been using for practice, talking in low tones. Jack put his hand on her arm and Ro jerked it away. "I know, Jack."

He shook his head and then saw Seraphina, saying. "There you are. I thought we could head into town. It'll give you both practice with cars and stoplights."

"I'll drive first," Ro volunteered. "And then we can stop for a bite and Seraphina can drive back."

"Ro," the warning clear in Jack's voice.

"What?" she asked, trying and failing to look innocent. "It'll be more fun than driving around and pulling over to change."

"It sounds fun to me," Seraphina lied. Driving through town made her insides quake.

"Come on, Jack. Live a little."

"Fine. But we're not going to be out long. I have things to do this evening," Jack said, giving in to his sister's smile.

Ro whooped and climbed into the driver's seat.

Seraphina scrambled into the back seat and fastened her seat belt as Ro cranked up the car. The music blared out of the speakers as Ro reversed down the driveway.

"Ro, slow down," Jack snapped, "Or I'll be driving home in an hour."

Ro grinned at him but lowered the pace of the car to only twice the speed limit. "Relax, Jack. We've got this." She grinned in the rearview mirror. "Right, Fi?"

Faking a confidence she was far from feeling, Seraphina said, "Absolutely."

***

The car lurched into the curb, jerking Seraphina forward as two teen boys laughed and pointed. At least she wasn't driving this time.

"Shit, Ro. Make sure you turn the car off before taking your foot off the clutch," Jack said.

"What?" Ro glanced back at Seraphina, a blush riding her cheeks. "You make it sound like I almost killed us."

Seraphina hid her smile with her hair while she fumbled with her seatbelt, thinking how nice it was that Ro wasn't perfect for once.

"You could've hit someone on the sidewalk," Jack persisted.

"I didn't, Jack." Ro bit the words out, the smell of the sea rising in the confines of the car.

"But you could have." He leaned over the center armrest, his face more serious than Seraphina had seen since they started the lessons. "You have to be better than this, Ro. You know that."

Ro and Jack's glances clashed, and Seraphina's fingers stilled. The buckle wasn't the only thing choking her as salt and brine filled the car. Ro's eyes had turned a stormy white and brown froth to mix with the blue.

"I don't need you to tell me how to be, Jack. I'm well aware of my position," Ro said, her voice sounding as if multiple people were talking, but their tones were discordant to each other, clashing and harmonizing at the same time.

Seraphina had only ever heard her voice do that once, right before Ro had shut the bathroom door as she continued talking to someone on the phone. She'd stayed in the bathroom for four hours, not responding to Seraphina's knock or offer of snacks.

"Then act like it," Jack said, his voice thick with fatigue, as he stepped out of the car.

Ro stared at the empty seat for a moment, a myriad of emotions crossing her face.

"Is everything alright, Ro?" Seraphina asked into the tempestuous silence.

The storms leaked out of Ro's eyes, and her face slid into a neutral mask. One that Seraphina hated and had been seeing more than anything else recently.

Ro slid a pair of dark sunglasses on and said, "It's fine. Coming, Fi?" She left the car before Seraphina could respond.

It was not fine, not even close, but she had no idea how to help Ro when Ro stayed silent. Seraphina tugged and wiggled the clasp, swearing, until it popped free. She scrambled out of the car and followed the siblings into the cafe.

She wove her way through the tables, dodging umbrellas and servers to the table they'd secured right on the edge of the patio. The pair sat opposite each other, one facing the ocean and the other watching the other diners.

Seraphina slid into the seat between them and picked up the menu to give herself something to do. Hopefully, their mercurial mood shifts would kick in and this lunch wouldn't be as awkward as dinner.

At least the food would be edible.

"Hi, what can I get you to drink?" A perky server said, her ponytail swinging behind her.

"Water's fine," Jack said.

"Iced tea for me, please," Seraphina said.

"And for you?"

"A coke, thanks," Ro said, the words short.

The server nodded and left, stopping by the other tables as she did so.

"Do you know what you're having, Seraphina?" Jack asked.

The tension at the table hadn't eased. Seraphina's knee bounced while she scanned the massive menu.

"I'm not sure."

"You're not sure about a lot of things," Ro muttered.

"Roslynn!"

Seraphina buried her face in her menu. Since when did she become a target for Ro's anger?

"What? It's true. She can't decide on colleges, a major, where she wants to live, or what she wants for food. It used to be a running joke, but it's gotten old." The sound of disgust in Ro's voice made Seraphina want to curl in on herself, like she used to do when her grandfather yelled at her.

She wasn't that bad, was she?

*No.* The surge of anger that ran through her surprised her, and she closed the menu with a snap. "It's just lunch, Ro. So what if I haven't figured out my major? What does that have to do with you?"

Ro swung away, her eyebrows raised above her sunglasses. "Look who found her spine."

"Enough, Roslynn. You want to be pissed at me, go ahead, but don't take it out on her."

"I don't want to be pissed at you, Jack. I hardly see you anymore." She laid her arm across the table, her palm face up.

And there it was. The emotional shift Seraphina had been waiting for. Unfortunately, it wasn't aimed at her.

Jack's jaw clenched, but then he reached out and held her hand. "I know. Growing up sucks."

A chuckle masking a sob escaped Ro. "It does indeed."

The server interrupted the moment by dropping the drinks on the table. "Have you decided what you'd like to eat yet?"

Ro and Jack let go, sliding back in their chairs like two guilty lovers caught in the act.

Seraphina found it odd until she remembered Ro's parents hardly ever touched each other in the house, let alone when they ate out. What was it about expressing affection that was forbidden? Or was it a Merrowfolk thing?

"Of course," Ro said. "I'll have the fish and chips."

"Same for me."

The server turned expectantly to Seraphina. With a glare at Ro, Seraphina said, "The roast beef au jus, please."

Ro shrugged, a small smile tugging at her lips, as if Seraphina amused her.

Gods, she was so sick of this. The turmoil of the table cut through Seraphina, and she turned to watch people playing volleyball on the beach, glad her sunglasses hid her eyes. She wouldn't say another word about anything if that's how Ro wanted to play it.

"Seraphina, what options are you thinking about for a major?"

Seraphina shifted her gaze back to Jack, her vow to be silent tested in its first minute. *Screw it.* "I'm not a science person, can't draw or do art, suck at math, and the only thing I'm good at is reading. It doesn't leave a lot of options." She winced as Ro laughed. "Forget I said that. I'll figure it out."

She stabbed the ice in her cup with her straw. She should've gone home. At least there, she and her aunt could've avoided each other instead of being tortured over meals like a period piece with her as the poor cousin they only invited out of pity.

"Well, if it's any consolation, I didn't know what I wanted to study until halfway through my second year. Even Beatrice's threats couldn't make me choose. But when I did, it was like putting on a second skin."

"Or a third," Ro quipped.

"Pick a school and decide your major when you know for sure."

Seraphina smiled at him, grateful he didn't react to her surly attitude. He was only ever nice to her, unlike his sister. "I at least have an idea for what school I want, so yeah, maybe I'll register as undecided and go from there."

She glanced at Ro to see if a snarky comment about school choices was incoming, but Ro's attention was focused elsewhere. Seraphina followed her stare to the rowdy crew who jostled their way through the tables toward them.

"Hey, Grifs, Jack," Samson called out as they hit the table, the other three boys fanning out behind them.

"Samson. It's been a while. I didn't expect to see you here," Jack said, an undertone in his voice that Seraphina couldn't place.

Samson's posture didn't change, but the three boys behind him stiffened as if slapped. "Can we join you guys?" Samson asked, dipping his head as if asking for a favor. "They're out of tables and we're starving."

Jack opened his mouth to speak, but Ro cut him off. "Of course. There's plenty of room. Grab some chairs." As the boys scattered, Ro leaned across the table and said quietly, "It's cool, Jack. We partied with them a couple of weeks ago and they were generous." They shared a glance with plenty of crosscurrents to it, none of which Seraphina understood.

Jack sat back and played with his napkin. "Fine, but we're not partying with them today. I have an important meeting to prepare for tomorrow."

Ro grinned back at him.

A ripple of unease stole through Seraphina. She had a feeling he wasn't going to get his way, however much she wanted him to.

# 10

## PEDALS AND TREES

### (DRIVING WASN'T FUN ANYMORE)

The hiss of the engine filled Seraphina's ears. Heavy pressure on her chest made it hard to breathe. Her head felt cracked open and throbbed as if someone stabbed it with a knife, over and over again. She pushed herself away from the steering wheel, careful not to move too fast.

The afternoon went pretty much how Seraphina had expected. The boys ordered a beer, and it wasn't long before Ro drank it too. When Jack had protested, she reminded him that Seraphina could drive. It hadn't taken long for Jack to concede having a beer as well, especially as Ro told funny tales, getting the table roaring in laughter.

Jack's metabolism should've kept him from getting too drunk on the few pitchers of beer they all drank between them. But then Ro ordered shots, and it all went downhill from there. One hour bled into four and the sun sank from the horizon as they finally stumbled out of the bar.

A warm, wet trickle slid down her face, but she ignored it. She checked on Jack in the passenger seat, but it was empty. The world smeared around her, and she put her head back until it stopped.

A groan rose from the back seat.

"Ro, are you alright?" Seraphina asked, the seatbelt digging into her stomach stopping her from turning around. She pushed on the clasp but couldn't seem to make it work. She tried to put her feet flat on the floor for better leverage, but she couldn't get her left foot free.

*Dammit.*

"I'm fine. Only bruises." The sound of a bottle hitting metal under the seat made Seraphina jump a little, and she tugged harder at the clasp.

"Jack's not in the car, Ro."

"Shit. Did he get ejected?"

Seraphina's breath whooshed out of her as she took in the damaged windshield. Cracks covered it, the tree in front of them fractured in the slivers of glass.

"No. Not through the front, anyway." She tugged harder on the belt. It was all her fault. "I can't get my stupid seatbelt off."

The back door opened, the car shifting as Ro slid out of the car. She swore and then opened Seraphina's door. "This is bad, Fi. We've killed the car."

The tree, now enmeshed with the car hood, agreed with her. "I think we killed the tree too," Seraphina said, her voice shaky. "Find Jack, Ro. Now."

"I'm sure he's fine. We're made of tougher stuff. This car, though, is not so tough."

"Everyone alright?" Jack asked, his voice tense and coming from the right.

"Yeah, but Seraphina's stuck."

"Fuck." Jack wrenched the passenger door over and leaned across the seat, his face scratched, and his shirt torn. "Where are you stuck?"

"Just the seatbelt, I think. I don't know. My foot is jammed near the clutch, but I think I can get it out once I can get out of the gods damn seatbelt!" Seraphina yelled, yanking on the belt.

"Let me. Seraphina," Jack said, his voice calm and even, "Let me try."

Tears slid down her face as she sat back. "I'm so sorry."

"It's not your fault."

"Yes, it is. I was driving."

"But you shouldn't have been." He broke the seatbelt holder, the strength of his bloodline showing the simple movement as he slipped it off her.

Seraphina bent down to check her foot. It hurt less than her head, so it was probably fine.

"Ro, help Seraphina get unstuck."

Ro blinked a few times. "Okay. But if I bend down too far, I may throw up."

"I'm sorry, Ro."

"It's fine, Fi. We're fine. It's going to be okay."

Seraphina's voice shook as more tears fell. "No, it's not. I ruined the car. I almost killed you both. It's so not okay."

Ro knelt and slid her upper body into the footwell. "Focus, Seraphina," she snapped, as the cold shock of her fingers touched Seraphina's ankle.

Seraphina took a shuddering breath and released it. "What do you need me to do?"

"I'm going to push your foot, so follow the direction I go. It doesn't look broken, but it's really jammed. "

"Got it."

After a few moments of swearing from them both and a sharp pain, they pulled her ankle free. Ro slid out of the footwell and sat back on her knees. Seraphina swung her legs around to the outside of the car, wiggling her ankle around. It hurt, but she had full movement.

She let out another shaky breath and asked, "Now what?"

Jack came around to the driver's side and put his hand on Ro's head. "You good?"

"Yeah, just bruised."

"How's the foot?" Jack asked.

"I think it's okay. It's sore, but not broken. We'll see how it is when I stand up," Seraphina replied, her teeth shattering from shock. The wind shifted and blew her hair around her face.

"Where are you bleeding?" Jack asked, his voice sharp.

Seraphina blanched when she touched the sore spot on her forehead, some of her hair stuck in the blood. "My head. I hit it on the steering wheel."

"Fuck." He ran his hands through his hair. "Anybody got their phones? I lost mine in the bushes."

Ro checked her back pocket and pulled hers out. "It's Roslynn. We've had an accident. We're on Magnolia Lane, just down from the bend. Come get us and bring a tow for the car." She ended the call with no one saying anything on the other line. "He'll be here in five minutes."

Ro and Jack shared a grim look. "If Beatrice wasn't here– "

"Then this wouldn't be a problem, but she is. Besides, had Seraphina not been here, it would've been even less of a prob-lem."

Tears rushed back into Seraphina's eyes. "I'm sorry. I'm so sorry. I ruined your summer."

"No, you ruined yours," Ro said, her voice harsh.

"Roslynn," Jack growled.

"What? I'm being honest. She would've found a way to pun-ish me, no matter what Seraphina did. Now, she has good cause and an empathetic picture," Ro waved at Seraphina, "upon which to base it."

"I don't understand," Seraphina said, exhaustion swamping her.

"You don't have to understand. It's not your place to," Ro snapped.

"Roslynn!"

"What?"

Before he could answer, the glare of oncoming headlights hit them. Seraphina raised her arms to cover her eyes, but her head still exploded a little. The SUV pulled over and Dannings climbed out.

"Everyone alright?"

"Yes. Seraphina is dinged, but fine," Ro answered, her voice sounding more like Beatrice's than her own.

"Good. Get in the car. I'll help Ms. Lastra and then be back to tow this mess to the house."

Seraphina stood, her hand on the door frame to keep her steady. Warm tingling raced up her spine and into her head, a sensation that felt familiar somehow. She frowned, trying to place it.

Dannings slid next to her and held out his arm, and she stopped thinking of the past and focused on what came next. A potentially horrible step. She wrapped her arm around his and put weight on her injured foot, the breath hissing out of her, turning to a sigh of relief as the pain stayed at its current level. They walked at a slow pace to the waiting vehicle and Dannings helped Seraphina into the back seat.

He climbed into the driver's seat, hung a U-turn, and drove sedately up the hill to the house. The movement outside the window made her nauseous, so she closed her eyes and waited for the car to stop.

Ro's sharp indrawn breath let her know that they'd reached the house. Beatrice stood on the top step, her mouth a tight line. Lights blazed from every window and Dorothy lurked behind Beatrice, waiting to be of service.

Dannings opened Seraphina's door and helped her out as Ro and Jack stepped out on the other side.

"Explain yourselves," Beatrice said, ice dripping from words.

"The car hit a tree," Jack said.

As Dannings brought a limping Seraphina around, Beatrice's eyebrows raised and she glared at Jack and Ro, who stood side by side, their shoulders touching in solidarity.

"A deer ran out. I swerved and lost control," Seraphina said in the silence. "I'm sorry."

"Fi," Ro warned.

"What? It's my fault. I could've killed you all. I'm the one to blame."

"Seraphina, this is the part where you don't understand, and you don't need to. Stop talking," Ro's voice shattered the still night air, the tone colder than the ice rink at school.

Seraphina blinked at her.

"You have been injured. You will go into the house and get treatment. Dorothy, call the healer," Beatrice said. Dorothy nodded and disappeared back into the house. "Dannings, take her inside and then go deal with the wreck. Where did it occur?"

"Two miles down the road before the Jennings' estate."

"Good, then no one will see it."

As Seraphina entered the house, she heard Beatrice say, "What do you have to say for yourselves?"

Dannings kept moving them forward, so she couldn't linger to hear what happened next, but it didn't matter.

She'd already ruined everything.

# 11

## THE STILLNESS OF GLASS

### (Everything Was Broken)

Seraphina sat near the window, her bruised foot on a stool and an open book on her lap. She stared at the drive and the yard beyond, but didn't see it, her mind spinning on everything that had come to pass. It had been three days since the accident. After Dannings had escorted her upstairs to her room, she had heard shouting and then eery silence, as if everyone had left.

The healer had arrived and tended to her injuries, which were more minor than she had feared. She had a slight concussion, and a bruised ankle, the healer prescribing rest and calling the healer back if her nausea or headache worsened. The healer had said something odd, though. She had said it appeared as if Seraphina's head had begun to repair itself, based on the aether swirling around it.

Seraphina had shrugged it off as being a human born of Shifters. Any other explanation made her uncomfortable. Besides, she wasn't special. Everyone said so.

A sharp knock sounded on the door and Seraphina said, "Come in." Her mouth dropped open when Ro wandered in, her skin pale and her eyes burning as if she'd had a fever. "Ro!" she said as she pushed the book to the side and scrambled to get up.

"Don't get up. I'm not staying long," Ro said, her voice flat. "Are you alright?"

"I'm fine. Are you?"

"Good," Ro replied, avoiding Seraphina's question.

"Ro."

"I need to sleep and eat and..." Her voice trailed off.

"Is Jack okay?"

Seraphina had seen no sign of either Ro or Jack since that night and anytime she asked Dorothy, the woman remained tight-lipped and silent.

"He's fine. He's back in the city." Ro's voice sounded hollowed out, the echo of her sadness mingling somewhere in the vacant tone. "Vacation over."

"I'm sorry." Tears rushed to the surface. She'd ruined his summer too.

"Don't. Don't you dare." The tide had turned, Ro's voice low and dark. "I didn't spend three days in hell to face your weepy bullshit."

Seraphina's mouth dropped open. "What do you want me to say, then?"

"Nothing. I want you to say nothing to me ever again."

Ro's wrath washed over her, and Seraphina struggled to breathe.

*Oh gods. I've broken us like I broke the car.*

How did she fix this? Her mind jumped from one solution to the next, tossing them out as soon as she thought of them. Panic gripped her as her best friend walked away, as if every step pained her. But Ro didn't hesitate once.

Nothing could fix this. Ro would only see pain when she looked at Seraphina. Only one choice remained. "I'll make my way back to school or Merricott tomorrow."

Ro wheeled around, her face a mask of anger. "No. You will stay here the entire summer and return with me to school. You do not get to run away from this."

"I'm not running. You don't want me here!"

"It doesn't matter what I want. If I got what I wanted, you and I would never have been friends, never have even met."

Seraphina's heart clenched so hard it felt like Ro had stabbed it. "Then why should I stay?"

Ro hissed out, "You agreed. If you don't, I'm the one who takes the hit, not you. Never you." She closed her eyes for a moment and when she opened them, all color had been leached out of them, leaving only murky darkness. "Keep your word and I'll keep mine. We'll interact at family dinners and play nice for Beatrice."

A wave of emotions swam through Seraphina, bitterness riding the crest. "Fine. Have it your way, you always do."

They glared at each other, the space between them as big as an ocean.

"You don't get it. And you never will." Ro's words lingered in the air as she walked out the door.

It closed with a click, and Seraphina put her head in her hands and cried.

***

Seraphina hugged her knees closer to her. A week had passed. The silence between her and Ro had stretched out so far, she didn't know if they'd ever breach it. The pain of losing her best friend hadn't lessened, but it helped that they only ever saw each other in passing. Ro appeared so lost and miserable that she wanted to grab Ro and shake her.

Or hug her.

Seraphina wasn't sure from one minute to the next how she felt about anything. She'd taken to spending her mornings in the library, reading, that same chill pulling books out at random, which she dutifully piled on the table near the window, all aspects of resistance gone. The afternoons she spent on the beach, walking, sitting, and crying, where no one could hear her.

And every other day she had a driving lesson for an hour by herself with Dannings. He also taught her how to control a slide by taking her on the sand and making her do donuts. She would've enjoyed it if it were anyone else besides him. But at least he was kind to her.

He was the only person in the house to speak to her since Ro had closed the door. And even that was only instructions. A wall of glass separated her from everyone else, as if she'd fell asleep and woken up somewhere else. She'd read a book like that once. She now knew how the character felt.

Soul crushing.

Ro was right about one thing, though. Seraphina had brought it on herself.

A lifetime of regrets and doubts assailed her like the wind blowing her hair around, tugging her one way and another. She'd spent so much time making herself small and invisible, she didn't know who she was anymore. Ro had filled the space between them with her giant personality and wicked sense of humor. Until she hadn't.

Seraphina squeezed sand through her fingers as it sank between the gaps she couldn't see. She wished she could say the same about the fractures between her and Ro. When she reviewed the last year, she could see the cracks weakening their friendship, but not the reason for it, nor even when they had started.

Searching her memories hadn't helped. She'd even tried journaling and ended up ripping it out in disgust. She could see the markers; they littered her memories like signposts on the side of the road. A fake laugh here, a silence there. The new friends she'd hated before now filling Ro's time. The manic laughter and crazy energy spilling over into everything Ro did.

Knowing when they happened fixed nothing, though. Not with Ro and not with her. She'd request a new room and finish out the school year. One last year of not existing except for class and then she'd be free.

She would spend the time figuring out what she wanted to do with her life and move on from this one. It was time to stop running from her problems and face them head on.

# 12

# THE DECISION WAS MADE

## (PROMISES, PROMISES)

Seraphina sat in the library's stillness, an old book on her lap. Her fingers explored the leather, cracked in places. When she opened it, a few pages fell out, the seams cracked and broken. She slipped them back in, sad at the destruction of such a beautiful book. She wished she could fix it.

Gods, she wished she could fix everything, but that wasn't her gift.

She flipped to the first chapter and more of the book cracked open.

*Crap.*

Maybe she shouldn't read this one. Or maybe... Tapping her fingers on the cover, she thought about the video she'd seen when she'd first arrived. She grabbed her phone and typed in a few search terms into her browser. A long list of articles and videos appeared on the screen.

Galvanized into action, she bounced out of the chair and dashed to her room to find her laptop. This could be it, the idea that had eluded her for the past year. A few hours later, with a notebook filled with notes, she sat back. She had a plan. The rightness of it filled up the hole Ro's leaving her had left.

A smile slid across her face, the first one to break through the gloom in two weeks.

She needed more research, though, so she rushed back into the library. Pulling books off the shelf and inspected them, she noted any volume with cracked spines, missing leather or covers that fell off. She wanted to understand the full depth of the issues to solve.

In the middle of inspecting *The Philosophy of Loyalty*, Seraphina sucked in a breath as Beatrice walked in and paused, a frown wrinkling her otherwise pristine brow.

Seraphina hadn't seen her since that horrible night, and she hadn't missed her either. Dread sunk deep into her stomach, her heart hammering in her chest as she took in the massive piles of books strewn around the room.

*Oh gods.*

"Whatever are you doing? I asked you to pick a few books, not all of them." Beatrice's tone could've cut through glass.

"I'll put them all back, I promise. I made a note of where they went," Seraphina stammered in response.

"That still didn't answer my question."

"Oh, right. Sorry. I am cataloging the different areas of a book that could be broken so that I can research how to fix it." Seraphina knew, as soon as the words fell out of her mouth, they were the wrong ones. Beatrice drew back and opened her mouth to speak, but Seraphina rushed on. "What I mean is, you have all these beautiful old books that have been loved and handled. That handling caused disrepair, but they can be fixed. And I think I can fix them."

*Oh gods.* That wasn't any better.

Beatrice's mouth closed with a snap. "Are you implying I do not know how to take care of my property?"

"No. Not at all," Seraphina lied. How did she get out of this one?

"Really? I beg to differ. I fear my hospitality has been misplaced, Ms. Lastra."

Beatrice using her last name sounded like a death knell. She scrambled to fix it. She didn't want to be the reason for Ro to be punished again. "It hasn't. I appreciate everything you've done. Truly. I figured out what I wanted to do, as a career, and my enthusiasm got the best of me."

"And insulting my library is part of that plan?"

"No. Not at all. I love your library. I love the books, the room, the way it smells, and how warm it is." The joy she felt in talking about the books took over. "That's not what this is about. This is about books and how easily they can get damaged. I want to restore them and make them like new, so that they can continue to be read after the glue has dried and cracked, or the leather has worn off."

Seraphina braced herself to be tossed out on the curb. If nothing else, she'd get away from the torturous silence. And she'd still have her plan. Neither of those thoughts kept the queasiness at bay, though. The tension built as she waited to be swept away in Beatrice's anger.

"Hmm. You may have a point."

Breathing as if she'd just run a marathon, Seraphina pressed the advantage. "I've been doing some research, and these can all get fixed. I think, I hope, I can learn to fix them."

She only wished she could do the same with Ro.

"How would you do that?"

"I've found a few master's programs that focus on textiles and conservation. I'd have to get a bachelor's degree first in English and then apply, but it could work." Seraphina shook her head.

"Ro, er, Roslynn was right about what I should major in, even if she was wrong about what I should do with it."

"My granddaughter has a lot to learn, including deciding for other people what they should do with their lives when she does not know the same for herself. It is a failing I intend to correct."

A fierce wave of protectiveness washed over Seraphina, the need to erase some of the pain she'd caused Ro driving her to say, "You're wrong about her. She knows what she wants. Being decisive isn't the problem." Seraphina bit back the words, "you are," and forged ahead. "You should see her when she's reading her biology textbooks. She's consumed by them like I am with literature."

Beatrice drew herself up. "I am never wrong. I know my granddaughter much better than you. Roslynn doesn't study as hard as she plays. If she had, maybe then she'd see the value in it and act accordingly. This business with the car, for example, would have never happened if she had."

"Roslynn had nothing to do with it. I crashed the car into the tree. I caused my injuries."

*And I will die on that hill, you malicious old biddy.*

Beatrice's mouth puckered as if she could hear what was left unsaid and found it bitter. "You are incorrect, but that is of no matter." She reached over and picked up a book off the top of the pile, the spine separating as she opened it. Disgust rippled across her face. "Very well. You may stay, but only if you return the books to their rightful place and promise to use the skills you'll learn to fix the more important books in my library."

*Wait, what?*

The breath rushed out of Seraphina, and she nodded. "Of course. Thank you. It'll be awhile though; I have a lot to learn."

"You do indeed, and not only about mending books." Beatrice dropped the book on the floor and sauntered out, the faint lingering of salty air following her. Over her shoulder, Beatrice said, "Dinner is at seven pm sharp. Do be on time."

"Yes, ma'am."

Seraphina sat back and wiped her brow. That had been close. Too close. She needed to take a page out of Ro's book and learn to think before she talked, especially around Beatrice. She glanced at the many books she'd get to fix, and she almost squealed in joy.

First things first, though. She needed to apply and get into a good school with the right master's program. It felt good knowing where her future lay.

She only wished she could tell Ro about it.

# 13

## THEY HAD TO STOP MEETING LIKE THIS

### (Seriously)

Seraphina stood in the mirror, frowning at her outfit. She glanced at the clock. It would have to do. She had nothing else, and she wasn't going to wear what Ro had lent her. Not now.

She wasn't even sure Ro would want her to after their fight.

Taking a deep breath, she left her room, her feet heavy and slow as if wading through deep water.

*Smile and nod. Keep it simple.*

Murmurs of conversation streaked through the hall, and Seraphina followed them to the living room. Ro's dad stood at the bar, mixing drinks, while Ro and her mom lounged on the sofa, chatting. All sounds ceased as Seraphina entered the room, broken only by the rush of a cocktail filling a glass.

"That's an interesting choice for dinner attire, Seraphina," Rowena said, her tone neutral. "I would've thought Roslynn would've lent you some of her clothes if you didn't have the right attire."

"I did. She obviously chose not to wear any of them," Ro said, her face a mask of icy stillness.

Rowena glanced at Ro.

Dinner wasn't going to suck; it was going to be torture.

"You've all been so generous that I didn't want to be a burden," Seraphina said, the words falling in the hush that followed.

"Nonsense. You still have ten minutes. Go upstairs and change immediately. My mother would not appreciate the disrespect your clothes insinuate," Rowena said.

Ro smirked and said nothing.

"Okay. I'll be quick." Seraphina pivoted on her heel and ran up the stairs, trying and failing to keep the tears from spilling over. She stripped, leaving the clothes in a pile on the floor, and pulled out a simple sheath dress that covered her shoulders and fell to the floor. Two minutes had passed. She swiped at her cheeks and pinched them, the pain stopping the tears.

*I can do this. Smile and nod.*

It felt as if something had died inside her every time she looked at Ro, so she needed to not look at Ro. She nodded once at herself in the mirror and rushed back downstairs.

"Much better and right on time, too," Rowena murmured as Seraphina slipped onto a chair facing the windows.

Jefferson lifted the cocktail shaker at her.

"No thanks. I'll wait for the wine at dinner." She needed to be as sober as possible to get through this without crying.

"Suit yourself," he muttered, downing his drink in one gulp as Beatrice's footsteps could be heard in the hallway.

Beatrice entered the room. She glanced at each of them, a sour smile on her face at the cocktail in Ro's hand. Ro smirked and toasted her before taking a sip.

Rowena frowned, but said nothing.

"Shall we?"

Jefferson crossed the room and held his elbow out to Rowena as Beatrice swept from the room. Ro stood and set her glass down and asked without turning around, "Are you coming?"

Swallowing hard, Seraphina nodded, and they walked side by side to the dining room, an ocean of unsaid things between them. She slid into place and waited to sit until Beatrice sat. Dorothy rushed to serve the first course.

Silence filled the room as they ate. Seraphina forced herself to eat more than she wanted to because she could focus on it instead of Ro or the empty chair beside her where Jack had sat before.

Dorothy removed the first course and set the second course down. Seraphina took a sip of wine, swirling it in her mouth to rid it of the fish taste. Beatrice picked up her fork and took her first bite. Everyone else followed her move.

Seraphina speared a few leaves on her own fork and put them in her mouth, chewing as quick as she could. The clink of silverware on porcelain and the rustling of cloth as Dorothy hovered nearby was the only sound in the room.

Beatrice set her fork down and said, "Seraphina tells me you enjoy science, Roslynn. Why have I never heard of this before?"

Almost choking on her salad, Seraphina took a sip of water.

Ro flicked her eyes at Seraphina and then back at her grandmother. "You didn't ask."

The clatter of a fork hitting the plate broke the tension and Rowena said, "I apologize. It slipped."

Beatrice nodded at her daughter before turning back to Ro. "I shouldn't need to ask for you to tell me about your studies. As it is, I had to find out from your friend, who described your studious nature not once, but twice."

*Oh gods.*

Rushing into the breach to protect Ro from whatever acid Beatrice was about to spew, Seraphina set her fork down and said, "It was the truth." She kept her gaze steady on Beatrice, but she could see Ro chewing out of the corner of her eye.

"I didn't say otherwise."

*But you implied it, you old sea hag.*

Beatrice dismissed her with a sniff. "What science do you enjoy in particular? I believe biology was mentioned."

"Biology is my favorite, although chemistry is interesting as well," Ro finally said.

"What do you think you will do with it?" Jefferson asked. When Beatrice glared at him, he shrugged and said, "I apologize for interrupting, Beatrice, but as this is the first time we've heard of Roslynn being interested in anything school related, I couldn't help myself."

What was wrong with these people? They acted as if they had no knowledge of what Ro did in school, but Seraphina knew the school sent progress reports. Didn't they read them? Seraphina was so focused on her internal pondering that she missed whatever tension played around her.

When Beatrice said, "Accepted," and everyone collectively relaxed, Seraphina had her epiphany. She really didn't know anything about how things worked in Ro's phylum, but she should've at least studied the books available in the library. Especially the etiquette book.

She bet it laid out all the rules of convention the family followed as if burned into them, just like the few rules Seraphina's family had followed for family dinnertime. Maybe then she wouldn't have stuck her foot in it as much as she had.

The thoughts spun around in her mind of their returning to the house after the crash and Ro telling her over and over, she needed to stop saying it was her fault. Before she could grasp what tied them altogether, Beatrice's voice cut through her thoughts like a buzz saw.

"Roslynn, are you going to answer your father?"

Ro stared at her plate. "I'm thinking about marine biology. I'd not only enjoy it, but potentially I could use it to study the more serious issues that plague us."

"And you think you could do this better than the Security Forces of the Free Folk? Their scientists are legendary."

"They work with limited data. I could get further," Ro said, lifting her gaze to her grandmother's, the challenge unmistakable.

One corner of Beatrice's mouth lifted. "Yes, I do believe you can."

Ro's eyes widened before focusing on the food again, her hand shaking a little as she took a bite of salad. Her gaze met Seraphina's over the table, and she frowned.

Seraphina dropped her gaze and forced more salad down her throat as Beatrice moved on to another topic.

Her stomach roiled from the salty food, but her heart lightened at finally doing one good thing for Ro, even if it was too late.

# 14

## SUN AND SURF

### (Everything Felt Lighter)

The sun warmed Seraphina's cheeks and the rush of the waves filled her ears and she smiled. She always loved the ocean. Maybe one day she'd live near it. Once upon a time, she and Ro had had a plan to own houses next to each other. She could still do it; it just wouldn't be next to Ro's.

Her smile faded, along with her enthusiasm.

Dinner had ended much like the first one. More seafood courses and general chatter between Beatrice and the rest of them. Seraphina had followed Beatrice up the stairs, feeling Ro's eyes on her the whole way, her judgment searing the skin between Seraphina's shoulder blades.

Who cared what Ro thought?

Seraphina grimaced. She did, and she probably always would. The water pounded the shore, the relentlessness of it taking her breath away. Life ebbed and flowed the same way. Seraphina had always felt like a piece of flotsam being tossed around the waves. Now she felt as if she rode them, at least in one aspect of her life. She could only hope it spread to the other parts as well.

Feet appeared to her right and Ro sat down, mirroring her pose. "There's nothing like the ocean," Ro said.

Seraphina said nothing, but a kernel of hope ignited. She quashed it. She didn't want to get too far ahead of what Ro sitting next to her meant.

Ro sighed. "You stuck up for me to Beatrice." A dark chuckle followed her words. "Beatrice."

"I didn't think the code of silence applied to Beatrice. Gods, nothing applies to Beatrice except what she deigns to apply," Seraphina said, her tone low. She held herself tight, ready for Ro to tell her to shut up. When it didn't come, she glanced at her, surprised to see tears hovering on Ro's lashes.

"You don't understand. No one stands up for me. Jack tried when he was younger, and she punished him for it. Hard. He never did it again, although he tries to help where he can. And my parents," her voice took on a bitter cast, "Well, you see what they do. They follow her every order and would never tell her no, even when it was about me."

She scooped up sand and let it trickle out of her fingers. "But you stuck up for me twice. Once when we first arrived and then again yesterday, even after I'd been such a bitch to you. You told her I had value. Intelligence. That I wasn't what she thought I was."

Seraphina stilled, worried any slight movement would startle Ro into bolting away from her. "I only spoke the truth."

"I know. And I love you for it."

The tears slipped over and spilled down Seraphina's cheeks. The hope she held to a flicker roaring to life. "I didn't understand, Ro. I think I do now. The dinner, the rules, the reason the accident wasn't my fault, even though it was. I needed to be beaten over the head with it, but I finally understand."

"The accident wasn't your fault. It was mine," Ro said, her voice heavier than a bucket of wet sand. "I should've never convinced Jack to drink and expected you to drive, to carry me as I played. You both paid a price I never wanted you to pay."

"Yours was higher than mine."

"It wasn't high enough. I had to take out all my self-loathing on you, even after you tried to take the blame. And then I paid a bigger price by alienating my best friend."

Seraphina glanced at Ro in surprise. She'd always thought Ro didn't see her the same way Seraphina saw her, mainly because Ro had friends that she'd known since birth. She'd made peace with it a while ago.

"I'm sorry, Fi. I should've never said anything like that to you. I should've holed up in my room and healed before we spoke, but I was so angry, at you, at Jack, at Beatrice, but most of all myself. I needed to lash out, and you were the closest victim." The tears slid down Ro's face. "Can you forgive me?"

"For what? Telling it like it is? I've been a jackass. I knew something was different between us this year and I didn't even ask if you were okay. All I did was focus on my own drama and I missed what was going on with you. You need to forgive me first."

"What are you talking about?"

Seraphina focused on the shimmering water, a gull flying over it, searching for food. "You pulled away this year. You snapped when you normally wouldn't and then you hung out with people you hated, partying harder than I have ever seen you. And I never asked you why."

Ro focused on the surf. "I didn't think you noticed."

"Well, I did. Sort of." Seraphina cringed. "I thought it was about me."

Ro laughed, a hint of darkness still lurking within it. "Yeah, you do that a lot."

"I know. I'm an asshole!"

"No, you're a teenager trying to figure things out."

"So are you," Seraphina protested.

"No, not in the same way. Fi, I'm older than you by a lot. I've seen more, done more. Manaan knows most of it not good. I keep forgetting how young you are."

Seraphina traced a ward with her toe, debating whether to ask her about it. *Screw it.* "What happened, Ro?"

Ro blew out a breath and nestled her chin on her arms. "Beatrice happened. She lined up a suitable mate for me. A guy I hated. She told me he was the best pick of the lot, and she didn't care that he put his hands on me."

"What? What are you talking about?" Seraphina's knees dropped as she swung around to face Ro.

"It's not that. It wasn't rape. Nothing like that." She glanced at Seraphina and sighed. "He shoved me up against a wall once and squeezed my boob. In the grand scheme of things, it was nothing, but it showed me what kind of guy he was."

"And Beatrice set you up with him?" The outrage Seraphina felt couldn't even be contained in the words she used. "How dare she do that!"

A wistful smile slid on Ro's face. "You forget, she can do whatever she wants. She's the grand poohbah of our little club. When I told her, do you know what she said?"

"I can guess. The stupid sea hag," Seraphina muttered.

"She said, 'Good. That will mean you'll breed.'" Ro snorted. "That's all she cares about, our people and new cubs."

"She's a total bitch."

"That too. But it's alright, Fi, you don't have to take her on. When I met Simon, everything worked out. He comes from a proper family, not as good as Blake, but good enough. She relented when I threatened to never have any babies if she forced me to be with Blake."

"You said that?" Seraphina's mouth dropped open. "I would've loved to be a fly on that wall."

"I shook the whole time."

"If it makes you feel any better, I wouldn't have been able to stand when I stuck up for you. My legs shook hard enough to shatter my kneecaps."

Ro's chuckle grew into a full belly laugh, which caused Seraphina to join her. They both flopped back, wiping tears from their cheeks. A companionable silence stretched between them as the laughter petered out.

Seraphina studied the clouds, searching for images or signs that they were alright. Only one way to know for sure. She took a deep breath and said, "I've drafted an email to Barlett, asking for a new room assignment."

"Delete it."

Ro's response came back so fast Seraphina almost missed it. But still... "Are you sure, Ro? Maybe it'd be good for you to have your own space."

"What, so you can be stuck with Vicki Seton?"

Seraphina shrugged. "Maybe."

"No. It's our last year. We're going out in style, together." She grabbed Seraphina's hand and held it.

"Phew. I really didn't want to room with Vicki. She smells like patchouli oil and it's noxious."

"She thinks it'll make her more attractive to the boys. She missed the memo on showering." That set them both off giggling again.

It would all work out. They'd have a glorious year, get into good colleges, and figure the rest out later.

Ro stood and yelled, "Race ya!"

The promise of the summer she thought they'd have beckoned as Ro took off like a shot. Seraphina ran after her, her feet light beneath her. Everything was right with the world again.

For a little while, at least.

**15**

# BEWARE THE GIFTS OF THE MERROW

## (SHE HAD TO WEAR SHADES)

Her pile of clothes looked so small strewn across the bed. She'd been attempting to pack, but her battered suitcase gave up its last gasp, the zipper breaking when she opened it. She chewed on her lip while she figured out what to do. Maybe they could delay the start of their journey with a quick trip to town for a new bag. Or maybe they had bungee straps she could use to hold it closed.

A sharp rap interrupted her reverie, and the door opened before she could say, "Come in." That alone should've given her the clue it wasn't Ro, but she was too intent on her current problem to think about it much.

"Why aren't you packed?" Beatrice demanded.

Seraphina wheeled around, her heart thudding painfully in her chest.

*Crap.*

Dorothy stood behind Beatrice in the hall, five books in her arms.

"Um, I'm almost done," she lied.

"Don't lie to me, child."

Seraphina's shoulders slumped. "I apologize. My suitcase broke as I opened it, and I was trying to figure out what to do. But I think I have a plan if you have rope I can borrow."

"Nonsense." Beatrice turned. "Dorothy, put those books down on the bed and get the trunk out of the attic. The one with the brown straps I stopped using a decade ago."

"Oh no, that's not necessary. I could always go into town and buy a new one," Seraphina protested. She'd passed her driver's license test at the same time as Ro, and they'd been fighting with each other over who drove when they explored the Hamptons over the last few weeks of summer. Ro almost always won. The stinker.

"That will not be necessary. I have an item I no longer use. You'll be doing me a service by taking it." Beatrice eyed the blue nylon case at Seraphina's feet. "Besides, that should have been put out of its misery a long time ago."

"Thank you," Seraphina said meekly. She couldn't win this fight no matter how hard she tried and besides, what did it matter if she took an old trunk?

"Second, these books are the ones I am willing to part with." Beatrice waved her hand at the books stacked next to her clothes.

"Oh, wow. Thank you. I only expected one or two at the most."

"We have a deal, Seraphina."

Seraphina's eyes widened, her brain scrambling to remember whatever it was she said she'd do. "Oh, right. I will fix those books you deem important in your library."

"Exactly. And I expect you to deliver on that agreement."

"I will."

"Good. I have more important matters to attend to, so I leave you in Dorothy's capable hands." She pivoted on her heel and walked away without saying goodbye.

Seraphina blinked after her, unsure what any of that meant. Maybe Ro would know. Curious which books Beatrice gave her, she picked up the one on top. *The Art of War: A Treatise.* She frowned, trying to remember why and when she'd set that book aside.

Cold air swirled down her arms, the book vibrating in her grip. She set it down and stepped back, her heart pounding.

*That did not happen. It's just a book.*

Maybe that was left over energy from Beatrice.

Dorothy came back into the room, dragging a trunk behind her. "Here we go. Now, you leave this to me, while you check to see if you've left anything behind. Dannings is already downstairs, loading Ms. Roslynn's things into the car, so time is of the essence."

Relief rushed through her as Dorothy place the books in the trunk. "Right. Of course." Seraphina checked under the bed and in the closet but knew she wouldn't find anything. There wasn't much to find.

Dorothy closed the trunk with a slam and wheeled it to the top of the stairs. Seraphina swiped her purse and sunglasses off the dresser, taking one last look around. Ro's chuckles carried up the stairs, causing Seraphina to smile. It sounded like a genuine laugh, not that wild version she'd heard from her at school.

When Dorothy stopped walking, Seraphina reached down to grab the other handle.

Dorothy said sharply, "Leave it. Dannings will come and get it."

"Right."

*Gods, she had to stop doing that.*

Seraphina tripped down the stairs into the sunlight of the open doors, sliding her sunglasses. Ro grinned at her, the heart-shaped lenses of her sunglasses giving nothing away.

"You ready?"

"Ready Freddy."

"Let's hit it. I told Dannings we'd drive, and he said it would have to be over his dead body."

Seraphina smiled and slid into the back seat. Dorothy followed Dannings out of the house as he carried Seraphina's trunk to the back of the SUV.

"What's that?" Ro asked.

"Oh, my suitcase broke, so your grandmother gave me an old trunk she'd not used in a while."

Ro raised an eyebrow and said, "Beware the Selkie bearing gifts."

"Really?" Seraphina lowered her sunglasses, her eyes wide. What did she agree to?

Ro's face remained serious for a moment, and then she burst out laughing. "If you could see your face! No. If she doesn't value it, it doesn't count."

Seraphina slid her glasses back up to cover her uneasiness over the books. But if she repaired the books at the house, maybe that'd make them even. It was an agreement, not a gift, right?

It didn't matter. Dannings got into the driver's seat and started the car. As they drove away, Seraphina turned to look at the house until they rounded the bend, and she could no longer see it.

Ro chuckled.

"What?"

"You've got to see this." Ro showed her a meme someone had posted to the school bulletin board, with the principal's face pasted in over the face that should've been there.

Seraphina burst out laughing as Ro grinned beside her. "I wonder how long that'll last."

"Longer than Barnaby wants it to."

Seraphina shook her head, still smiling, as she gazed out over the flashes of blue between the trees. It wasn't the summer she expected, but she wouldn't have traded it for the world.

# Author Notes & Appreciation

The story continues in...

**The Deep Space Between**
Available Now

***

If you'd like to stay updated on all the latest news for the Space Between series and want to get the free prelude, *The Prior Space Between*, please sign up for my newsletter: cassandracstirling.com/spacebetween-book0.

In *The Prior Space Between*, Seraphina navigates six snapshots from five years of her early life (ages 8-13), where being barred from entering her family's library or being bitten by a frightened Elf were the worst things that could have happened to her. Until they weren't.

Last but not least, something I never realized until I became an author is how important book reviews are. If you enjoyed this book, I would love it if you could take a few minutes to throw a few stars at it and leave a comment about what you liked and didn't like.

# About the Author

Cassandra Stirling is all about books. She reads them, edits them, writes them, reviews them, and throws them at the wall when they frustrate her. They also appear as key features in all the series she writes, whether as jobs for her protagonists, a love of reading as a hobby, or as literary quotes to teach someone a lesson. You could say she is immersed in them in all the ways that count.

You can sign up for her monthly newsletter on her website: cassandracstirling.com/spacebetween-book0.

Or hunt her down on social media:

 facebook.com/CassandraCStirling

 instagram.com/cassandracstirling

 goodreads.com/cassandracstirling

# Also By Cassandra Stirling

**Space Between Urban Fantasy Series**
*The Deep Space Between*
*The Dark Space Between*

**Merryton Mews Cozy Mystery Series**
*Poison and Pens  (Kindle Vella)*
*Holly and Havoc  (Kindle Vella)*